D1277071

Friends and Relations

Friends and Relations

A Collection of Stories
by Daniel Menaker

Doubleday & Company, Inc.
Garden City, New York, 1976

The following stories originally appeared, in slightly different form, in The New Yorker: "Grief," "Long Weekend," "Sic Transit," "Accommodations at Uncle Sol's," and "The Three-Mile Hill Is Five Miles Long."

"A Different Set of Rules" originally appeared, in slightly different form, in the August 1975 issue of Redbook magazine.

"Mole Hall" originally appeared, in slightly different form, in the September 1976 issue of Mademoiselle.

Four lines of lyrics from "Come and Get Your Love," words and music by Russ Ballard. Copyright © 1975 Island Music Ltd., 47 British Grove, London W4, England. Controlled by Ackee Music, Inc., for the U.S. and Canada. All Rights Reserved.

Portion of lyrics from "If I Were a Little Girl" sung by Tammy Wynette. Copyright © 1968 by Moss Rose Music, Inc. Reprinted by permission of the publisher. All Rights Reserved.

Library of Congress Cataloging in Publication Data
Menaker, Daniel.
Friends and relations.
Contents: Grief.—Circumstantial evidence.—A different set of rules.—Reunion. [etc.]
I. Title.
PZ4.M54Fr [PS3563.E46]   813'.5'4

ISBN: 0-385-03896-8
Library of Congress Catalog Card Number: 76-12053
Printed in the United States of America
First Edition

To my mother and father,
and to the memory of my brother

Friends and Relations

Grief

About six miles west of Great Barrington, Massachusetts, a man of twenty-one years stands beside a dead and fallen apple tree on the edge of a field of snow. His name is David. He has been chopping the tree up for firewood, but now he is standing and resting, leaning on his axe. He breathes heavily and evenly, making white clouds in the frigid January air.

He looks down at the axe and realizes for the first time that it is the same one he gashed his foot with thirteen years before. It was in the summertime—one of the many vacations and holidays he spent at his uncle's farm as a child. He had sneaked off to the woodshed after hearing his uncle say that some logs needed splitting. David had been barefoot, and he remembers blood pouring out of his wound as if some spring had been opened. He imagines blood on the snow and shudders slightly. He also remembers that in the fall his brother Mark used to climb the apple tree, which was old even then, and wait for him to pass underneath, so that he could throw apples at him.

In front of him, across the field, stands a huge red barn, where his uncle used to keep more than a thousand nesting chickens. David gathered eggs from the barn when he was much younger. The barn is empty now, except for an old hay wagon left from before his uncle bought the place, forty years ago. In back of him is his uncle's farmhouse, painted the same dark red as the barn. Part of the house was built in the early seventeen-hundreds. Inside, it is decorated with Mexican paintings and sarapes. A few of the paintings are by the radical artist Siqueiros, who was a friend of the uncle's during his activist days in the thirties and forties.

David looks up again, beyond the field, past the barn, to white mountains across the valley. The stillness is broken, for a few seconds here and there, by brittle gusts of wind in the trees, whose twigs click and snap like thousands of sparrow bones. Light snow begins to fall, and he goes back to his work.

David's uncle had been helping with the chopping earlier in the afternoon, but the cold and his seventy-seven years allowed him only a few hours of hard work. Since the beginning of October, when David left his parents' apartment in

Manhattan and came to stay at the farmhouse, the two men have repaired the slate roof, replaced the water heater, almost filled the woodshed with firewood, painted some of the bedrooms upstairs, and shored up the outbuildings.

Now, as dusk falls, the uncle sits in front of the fire in the living room, reading the *Daily World*. Everything is silent except for the rhythmic thunk of the axe outside. Directly above him hangs a portrait of his mother and father, who died within two months of each other fifteen years ago, both well into their nineties. The father's features—a large Jewish nose, a kind, open expression, and clear blue eyes—are repeated in the son's face and in the gaunt face of the grandson outside. But David stands six feet one, taller by seven inches than his uncle and grandfather.

Now it is four-thirty and nearly dark. David joins his uncle before the fire. They talk for a while about the day's news. The uncle has become outraged by corruption in Washington and tries to explain to his nephew that in a true Socialist system, whose advent in America he considers imminent and inevitable, such things could never happen. David calls his uncle an incorrigible utopian and says that people are people and that governments will always be corrupt. This elicits a long talk from the uncle about Marxism-Leninism and the dialectic in history.

The young man, only half listening, marvels at the old man's passion and conviction, even though they derive more from dogma than from reason. He takes a sort of comfort from his uncle's physical and philosophical endurance, from the familiarity of his ideas, like good old clothes. From the time he was very small, David can remember his uncle's voice rising with enthusiasm as he tried to make converts on chilly September evenings in front of the fireplace. The house, too, creaking every now and then as if to gird itself against the storm gathering around it, seems comforting in its age and soundness.

Before supper, David goes upstairs to shower and take a nap. He dreams that he is back in his parents' apartment. It is midnight in the dream, and a strong wind is blowing millions of still-green leaves from the trees in Central Park. There is a knock at the door. His mother opens it, and his brother Mark enters. Everyone is overjoyed to see him. He has been on some great journey, and he has brought gifts. To David he gives a silver knife whose blade pulses with colors; to his father he gives gemlike crystals that emanate an intermittent keening sound; to his mother he gives a nest made of rusty nails inside of which sits one blood-red egg.

Mark sits down on a couch, exhausted. He falls into a deep sleep. David and his parents become concerned and try to rouse him. Finally, they sense some horrifying presence waiting at the door. David knows nothing about it except that gray mist envelops it. Mark awakens. He stands up and stretches, and smiles warmly. David is astonished by the whiteness and evenness of his brother's teeth. Mark shakes hands with his family, David last. He walks toward the door, where the grisly escort waits for him. David wonders at his brother's bravery "to consort with such a one as that," as he says to himself in the dream. He wakes up terrified and shaking.

Supper is thick beef stew and red Spanish wine. The uncle grew to like Spanish wine when he served with the Lincoln Brigade in Spain. David is pensive during the meal, still shaken by his dream. After he washes the dishes, he and his uncle play chess in the living room. The uncle taught David chess when he was a boy of ten. When he was sixteen, David won his first game, and shortly after that he began to win regularly. Tonight, though, he loses twice in a row, and the uncle knows that something is wrong but says nothing about it.

Finally, David acknowledges that he has had another dream about his brother. He tells the uncle the dream. The uncle says that the dream reminds him of certain English ballads. David says that he can understand why people have often believed that dreams are imposed on the dreamer by some outside force. If he had any control, he says, he would not permit himself to have these dreams.

The two are silent for a while. They sit together staring into the fire, listening to the wind rush around the house as if trying to gain entrance. David's thoughts keep returning to the dream. He feels cold and his hands begin to sweat. He has an overwhelming urge to defecate but remains in his chair as if paralyzed. Memories that he has been trying to hold back begin forcing their way into his mind.

He remembers standing in the door of the hospital room after his brother's surgery and raising his fist as a semaphore for courage. He remembers his own cowardice, his inability to join his mother in her vigil at Mark's bedside, to help him cough up blood from his lungs. He remembers his sister-in-law clenching and unclenching her fists in the belief that as long as she did so Mark's heart would keep beating. He remembers watching a doctor shout at his brother as he slipped into a coma, and he remembers his brother's feeble response—a slight, slow shaking of his head, like a refusal, an abnegation. He remembers tubes and machines, one that made a rhythmic beep like a ship lost in fog far out at sea.

The memories well out faster and faster. Finally, he remembers his brother's face in death, his eyelids not quite covering his eyes, as if he were looking out for something attacking him from below, his mouth set in a faint hint of the once brilliant smile.

It is the memory of the smile that melts the horror into grief. David stands up, turns away from his uncle, and puts his hands over his face. "I am so sorry," he says, and, at last, he weeps. The uncle keeps his gaze fixed on the fire and does not say a word.

Later, David climbs the stairs again and lies down on his

bed without undressing. He spreads an old quilt, which his uncle has told him once belonged to his great-grandmother in Russia, over himself, and falls into a deep and blessedly dreamless sleep. The snow continues to fall all night, but in the morning a brilliant white sun rises which makes the mountains so glisten that it hurts the eye to look on them.

Circumstantial Evidence

"Whoops!" I half heard Jenny say as I woke up that Tuesday morning.

"They've got guns!" I said, or at least that's what Jenny later told me I said.

But then I was all the way awake, and I heard her say, "We don't have to worry anymore, Paul. I had an accident."

"What do you mean?" I said.

"Look," she said, raising the top sheet and blanket. There were a couple of bloodstains on the bottom sheet.

"Thank God," I said. She was three weeks late, and we had been walking around the campus like a couple of criminals awaiting execution. Every time I had started to have a good time or get down to some hard work, I would remember that Jenny might be pregnant, and my shoulders would bend forward as if a circus strong man had hold of my clavicle and was bending it as he would an iron bar. I had been sleeping ten or twelve hours a day, to get away from thinking about the fact that we had probably ruined our whole lives.

It was just before the Pill back then, and if you went to bed with someone in college, you were a sexual frontiersman. In fact, Jenny had wanted to spend the night with me ever since we started going together, in September. But I was so scared of being caught or getting her pregnant that I wouldn't let her, until I got drunk one night in February. (I think, but am not sure, that Jenny got me drunk.) We were careful about the days, but that isn't a very safe way, of course—look at all those row houses in Crotona stuffed with little saints' names. So after Jenny was a week late, at the end of March, we thought we were finished. If what happened that Tuesday morning hadn't happened, she was going to take the train into Philadelphia in the afternoon and get tested at the Sanger Clinic. But it happened.

I hugged Jenny and jumped out of bed and started dancing around the room naked. "You look pretty silly," Jenny said, laughing.

"I'd better get you to class," I said, slightly out of breath but still jiggling. I was a junior and in Honors, so I didn't have any classes, but Jenny was only a freshman and had eight-o'clocks on Tuesday and Thursday mornings.

"What are you going to do about the sheet?" she said after we got dressed.

"Just leave it; I'll take care of it later," I said.

We snuck out of the side door of the dormitory. It was against the rules then even to visit a boys' dorm (or a girls' dorm, if you were a boy), to say nothing of staying overnight, as Jenny had been doing. Nowadays, I hear, they share the toilets; all the fun has gone out of it.

I started my Lambretta, Jenny got on the back seat, and I drove up the ramp from the basement feeling like Marlon Brando in *The Wild One*. It was only about forty-five degrees, but neither of us noticed the cold, even at thirty miles an hour.

After Jenny and I had lunch, she went off to practice field hockey, or whatever it was she played in the spring, and I went to check my mailbox. In it I found a note; it said, "Please come to my office as soon as possible," and it was signed "W. C. H. Clothier, Dean of Men." Oh, God, we're finished, I thought. He knows.

As I walked toward his office, I tried to figure out what Water Closet Head might know, and all I could come up with was the sheet. I didn't think that anyone had seen us leaving the dormitory, so the evidence was only circumstantial, but it was very circumstantial. Clothier had managed to kick people out for far less, or at least that was what we had all heard. He liked to expel people, we thought. In the late forties and fifties, it was rumored, he had led the campus police personally through the large meadow in the south campus looking for early-fall or late-spring fornicators. I myself had presided over the Student Behavior Committee meeting in which he delivered the famous line "There is no biological necessity for sexual contact during the college years." And he disliked me in particular, I thought, because I had done so much agitating for changes in the rules.

"What can I do for you, Dean Clothier?" I said, lounging down into the chair across the desk from him.

"The House Director, Miss Davis, tells me that you had a girl in your room overnight last night, Paul," he said. He had on his thick glasses, and the light from his office window reflected off them, so that I couldn't see his eyes.

"I beg your pardon," I said, drawing myself up into a rigid position, as if I were shocked.

"Miss Davis has told me that the house mother in your dorm, Miss Welding, has evidence that you had a girl in your room last night," he said.

"That's preposterous," I said. "What kind of evidence?"

"I don't know," he said. "Miss Davis was too embarrassed to tell me."

"Well, it's pretty difficult to answer charges when the person who's accusing me doesn't even know the facts in the case."

"I'm not accusing you, Paul. I'm simply looking into the matter. I shall talk with Miss Davis this afternoon and find out her reasons for reporting you. Perhaps you could come to my office again tomorrow morning."

"That's fine with me," I said, "even though there's no point in any of this, since nothing happened."

I got up and was nearly out the door when Clothier called me back.

"Oh, by the way, Paul, aren't you going steady with someone?" he said.

"Going *steady*?" I said.

"Someone you see . . . A girl, a young woman—you know."

"Yes, I'm going with someone."

"Who?" he said. "Would you mind telling me her name?"

"Yes, I would mind," I said. "I don't see what on earth you need to know anyone's name for. I keep telling you, nobody was in my room last night."

"I see. Well, then, I'll see you here tomorrow morning."

"O.K., but this whole thing is ridiculous," I said, and walked out.

This is terrible, I thought, running down the hall. How could they have found out about the sheet? Elizabeth, the maid, would never have told on me.

I ran out of the side door, toward where my scooter was parked. I started it up and gunned it a few times, now feeling like Steve McQueen in *The Great Escape*—as if a thousand Nazis on motorcycles were after me. I raced back

23

down to the dorm. In my room, I saw that the bed had been made with clean sheets. I went looking for Elizabeth, and I found her vacuuming the parlor. As soon as she saw me, she switched off the vacuum cleaner.

"Oh, Mister Paul, I couldn't help it," she said.

I asked her what had happened.

"Well, you know, every Tuesday I change the sheets," she said. I did know, but I had forgotten. "Miss Welding always follows me around, sniffin' and pokin'. This morning we was in your room, and I went to lay back that sheet, and there it was. Lord have mercy, child, I thought she would fall out. But then she says, 'I must report this to Miss Davis,' and she struts right on out."

"Where are those sheets, Elizabeth?" I said.

"Oh, I took care of *them*," she said. "Don't you worry about them. They goin' to throw you out?"

"I hope not," I said. "Elizabeth, you are an angel." I leaned over and kissed her on the cheek. She smelled like cinnamon; I can still remember that.

"You better *leave* us women alone, boy," she said.

I went back to my room and changed into gym shorts, a sweat shirt, and sneakers. If I could account for that sheet, I figured, I would be O.K.

I ran out into the small woods in back of the dormitory and looked until I found a gravelly spot where nobody could see me. There, I sank down hard on my knees—like a desperate seminarian, I remember thinking. I also remember that it didn't hurt a bit. I stood up to inspect the damage. There wasn't enough, it looked like, so I sank down again, a little harder. After the second time, my knees were pretty well scraped up and bloody. Once again, I went back to my room, where I washed out the wounds, picking out small bits of gravel and stone that had become embedded in the flesh. I was very calm throughout all of this, as if it were happening to someone else. Finally, I changed back into my jeans, leaving the scrapes exposed, so that they wouldn't heal too fast.

That night, Jenny and I ate together in the dining room, and I told her about what had happened. All she had to do, I said, was make sure that her roommate would vouch for her presence in their room the night before. There wasn't any way they could catch her.

She seemed more worried about my knees than about either of us getting expelled. Just like a woman, except you can't say that any more. "Let me see," she said when we sat down in the commons room after supper. There were lots of people around, and I didn't think it would be a good idea to go rolling up my pants and baring my wounds like Coriolanus in the marketplace.

"I'll just have to look at them later, then," she said, leering at me.

"Listen, you can't come down *tonight*," I said.

"Why not?" she said.

"Why not? How can you say that? We have to be careful."

"But that's exactly what they want us to do, you know," she said.

"Well, they've succeeded—at least with me."

"I think you're too worried about this," she said.

"Too worried! I don't want to screw up everything I've—"

"Oh, they're not going to throw you out," she said. "First of all, they now have as little on you as they have on me, thanks to Elizabeth. Second, they don't *want* to throw you out. Your parents pay your tuition, you're going to get a fellowship, you play basketball and football. I think Clothier likes your kind more than you realize, believe me."

"That's easy for you—"

"And I'm spending the night with you. You're acting like an old banker or something, and I've got to get you straightened out." She got up and led me out the big double doors of commons like a teacher leading a kindergartner across an intersection.

"Well, the whole thing's your bloody fault anyway," I said as we got on my scooter.

"Quit muttering," Jenny said.

"Come in, Paul," Clothier said from behind his desk. For an instant, I wondered whether he ever went home at night. "Let's get this thing straightened out."

I had put on Bermuda shorts when I got up, so that my

knees would be visible. That must have looked odd to Clothier, since it was even colder that morning than it had been the morning before, and I was certainly the only person on the campus wearing shorts. Because of his glasses, I couldn't tell whether Clothier had noticed the scrapes. I had wanted him to see them and then do the explaining himself, but, as it turned out, he said nothing. As I walked across the room to the chair across the desk from him, I tried to sort of flash my knees without looking too much like a Clydesdale, but, I found out, that is very hard to do.

"I've spoken with Miss Davis again," Clothier said after I sat down, "and she was still very uncomfortable about discussing this matter. She did tell me that the girl you had in your room must have been a virgin, however, so I think I now have a clearer picture of what we're dealing with here."

"Maybe this will give you an even clearer picture," I said. I stood up abruptly, like a soldier coming to attention, and knocked over the chair as I did so. I pointed both index fingers down toward my knees but kept looking at Clothier, the way you do in that silly dance step from the lindy, or whatever it is. "I was jogging on the cinder track around the football field on Monday evening, and I fell. I didn't put bandages on, because I thought they would heal faster if they were open. Anyway, that's where the stains come from, if that was what Miss Davis was talking about. In fact, maybe I'll get turned in again this morning; there are more stains." That part was true, and I felt extremely indignant for a moment. I turned around and righted the chair. "I guess that takes care of that," I said as I sat down again. "Unless there's some other 'evidence,' which there couldn't be, since nothing happened, as I told you yesterday." I was now feeling panicky, and my voice kept breaking. It sounded almost as if I were yodeling. Clothier sat there very calmly.

"I see," he said. I was sure that he didn't believe me at all. *I* certainly wouldn't have believed me. "Why were you jogging?" he said. "Don't you play baseball?"

"No, just football and basketball. I like to keep in shape, though. I don't like to let myself go just because it's spring. Anyway, what difference does it make why I was jogging? I was jogging."

"I see," he said again. There was a long silence. I wanted to rip his eyeglasses off and trample them.

"Well, I've got some studying to do," I said finally. Sliding the chair back carefully, I got up again and walked toward the door. When I got there, I turned around. "I hope you're satisfied about this whole thing," I said. Clothier still said nothing. "Listen, what Miss Davis said was pretty slanderous," I said. "Somebody owes me an apology."

"I think that's going a bit too far," Clothier said. He was smiling.

I found myself smiling back. "Yeah, I guess maybe it is," I said, and walked out.

After that, I actually did start jogging around the cinder track, to sort of shore up my alibi, in case anybody was watching. Once, I even had the satisfaction of seeing Clothier walk by, although he was too far away for me to be able to tell whether he recognized me. I've been jogging ever since. It really is terrific exercise; I'm up to a few miles a day now—twice around the Central Park reservoir. Sometimes Jenny gets mad; she says that I'm being compulsive and that running takes up too much of my time.

A Different Set of Rules

Ben was walking down the stairs from the commons room above the dining hall. A girl with a bandage over one eye was walking up. Ben stood on the landing and watched her ascend toward him. She would not meet his eyes, but kept her head forward. Like a soldier in drill, Ben thought.

"So you're the one," Ben said as the girl reached the landing. She stopped and turned to face him, and smiled broadly.

"Yes," she said, "I'm the one." She was a short but substantial girl, with ample hips and square shoulders. She had wide cheekbones and a full mouth with even, very white teeth. Her forehead was broad, and her hair was straw-colored and boyishly short. Her unbandaged eye, large and blue-gray, like a clear, cold solitaire, was so beautiful that Ben had to look away.

"I read about you in the *Phoenix* this morning," he said, surveying the line of students at the foot of the stairs outside the dining room. "Is it going to be O.K.?"

"The patch comes off tomorrow," she said.

"Good," he said, forcing himself to look at her again. "That whole Freshman Serenade thing is pretty tribal, anyway."

"Oh, I don't know," she said.

"You mean you enjoyed getting thrown around in the mud by a bunch of jocks?"

"Until I got kicked," she said, and giggled. "Anyway, you're a jock yourself."

She knew who he was. He felt pride wash through him like strong liquor, and he blushed. "Not that kind of jock," he said. "I just can't understand how you could like getting pawed that way."

"What kind *are* you, then?" she said.

"I eschew categories," he said, self-mockingly. "Just because I play soccer doesn't mean I have to play soccer with a girl's face." He paused. "I read your name, but I've forgotten it."

"Stephanie McCullough. People call me Stevie."

"I'm Ben Jaffe."

"I know."

"Well, if it's as pretty as the other one, I can't wait to see it," Ben said, gesturing toward the bandage.

"Oh, it's even prettier."

Ben laughed. "I'm on my way to lunch," he said. "I want to finish in time to see Kennedy. Have you eaten already?" His own invitation took him by surprise, which was what he wanted, so that it would seem casual to himself as well as to her. But his heart like a traitor started pounding almost immediately.

"No, I already have," she said.

"Maybe some other time," he said quickly. "Well, so long. I hope—"

"I would look forward to it," she said.

"I hope that you're O.K." He backed down a couple of steps. "Keep an eye out for me," he said, and shrugged apologetically.

Ben met his friend Jed Cooper in the dining room, and after lunch they strolled together down the wide, oak-lined walk that split the college's spacious front lawn in two. It was a bright, early-October Friday afternoon, genial and comfortable in the sun, but a little chilly in the deep, sharp shadows of trees and buildings. Every now and then, a vortex of leaves swirled around the feet of the two young men as they walked. Nearby, the college maintenance crew was burning a big pile of leaves. The smoke drifted across the walk, at one point so thickly that it made Ben's eyes sting.

"We'd better hurry up," Ben said as they reached the railroad tracks that lay at the foot of the campus and divided it from the small college town. He could see the crowds that had already formed on the sidewalks of the town's main street. "I want to get a good look at this glamour boy."

"You rich Northerun fellahs always in a rush," Jed said, exaggerating his natural Kentucky drawl. He was tall and slim, like Ben, but he was also lanky and slow, while Ben was contained and tense. Their friendship, like their physical appearance, was a mixture of complement and contrast. They were both juniors and both studying in the Honors program. Ben was majoring in English, Jed in physics. They were both good athletes. Ben found his friends mainly among those students who considered themselves bohemians; Jed belonged to a fraternity. In the limited, idyllic world of a small Quaker college, both of them received wide admiration.

"I met the best-looking girl in the freshman class today," Ben said as they crossed the tracks. "I think I'll ask her to the movies tomorrow night."

"What's her name?" Jed said.

"You know, that one who hurt her eye in the Freshman Serenade Wednesday and got written up in the paper this morning. Stevie Something."

"McCullough," Jed said, "and she respectfully declines your kind offer."

"What are you talking about?"

"Well, she can't go to the movies with both of us, now, can she?" Jed said, grinning evilly, like a Halloween pumpkin.

"You son of a bitch," Ben said.

The motorcade, moving quickly in dappled sunlight, came into view half a mile down the road from the town. It slowed when it reached the edges of the crowd. The first few convertibles carried mainly nondescript, paunchy men, who Dave assumed were local Democratic officials. The fourth open car—as long and sleek as a boat—carried John Kennedy and his wife. The Senator stood to greet the crowd, waving with one hand and balancing himself by holding on to the back of the front seat with the other. He had a yellowish suntan and seemed slightly stooped. He was extremely handsome. For an instant, Ben met his eyes. His throat tightened, and he shivered a little. Then the car had passed, and the crowd's cheering first diffused and then died entirely, as if quenched by the hollow silence that took its place.

It was Sunday morning, and Ben was in his room, reading. He did well in all his studies—a success that he attributed to not much more than discipline and stubbornness. If a concept resisted him, he assaulted it relentlessly, first from this position, then from that, until it yielded.

"Was she hot!" Jed said loudly as he opened the door to Ben's room. He walked to the bed and fell onto it face down.

"Come on in," Ben said.

Jed turned over, flinging his arms and legs over the sides of the bed, and rolled his eyes up into his head.

"Listen, I've got some work to do, if you don't mind," Ben said.

"You wouldn't be jealous, now would you?" Jed got up. "Actually, you're golden," he said, losing his manic expression.

"What do you mean?"

"She knew we lived on the same hall. All she did was ask about you—where you're from, what you're like, why you dress like some kind of refugee. It was disgusting."

"Are you serious? That's terrific!"

"Of course, I felt obliged to tell her about your liaison with the old nigra chambermaid." Jed got up and went toward the door. "Are you going to lunch?"

"Just a second," Ben said. He got up and straightened his desk, taking care, before he closed his book, to underline the passage he had been working on. He put on his green deck coat and walked into the hall. Jed was already outside. Ben walked out the dormitory's side door into the bright sunlight. Whooping and screeching as if in a panic, he ran to catch up with his friend. When he did, he jumped up onto his back, nearly knocking him over.

Ben put his hands on the back of Stevie's skirt while he kissed her. As if in one of those oriental disciplines that hover between ballet and violence, she raised her arms up under his and opened them outward, pulling his hands away from her. He placed them high on her ribs, just touching the sides of her breasts. She held his wrists and leaned toward him, so that his hands finally rested on her back.

It was the end of their first date, a week after they had met. At Jed's invitation, they had gone to a dance given by his fraternity. Now they were standing under a lamppost outside Stevie's dormitory. The weather had turned quite cold, and Stevie shivered a little as a gust of wind swept past, pulling a rain of leaves down around them. She tilted her head back and looked at Ben. "You go pretty fast for a first date," she said.

"I'm sorry. It's just that I find you irresistible."

"Oh, sure."

"Listen, I really am sorry. I didn't mean to rush you or anything. But I do like you."

"I like you too," Stevie said, slipping away from his embrace. She took his hand and started walking toward the dormitory's entrance. "It's just that—"

"I know, I know," Ben interrupted. "We've only just met."

She tried to hit him, but he danced away.

Over the next few weeks, Ben saw Stevie as much as he could. He went to the registrar's office and looked up her course schedule, so that he could be wandering by in the hall when her classes let out. He would make sure that she saw him, and then, if she failed to approach him, he would pretend to discover her. When they did not have supper to-

37

gether, he would wait for her outside the dining room. Then they would go upstairs to commons, or sit and talk on the main building's front porch, or walk together down to the library.

Before September, Stevie said, she had never known a Jew. Her family was Episcopalian and so was she ("A believer," she called herself), and they lived just outside Tacoma, Washington. Her father, whom she admired very much, was the senior vice-president of a gigantic lumber company ("It's a cartel, you know," Ben said). He had been very unhappy about her going East to college. Her world in the West had been made of skiing trips, clamming in Puget Sound, square dances, golden retrievers (thinking about her dogs was one of the few things that made her homesick, she said), and two "pesky" younger brothers.

Challenged by such innocence, Ben found himself playing up the differences between their backgrounds. He mentioned casually that his parents had been radicals during the thirties and forties. He told her that his father, a Jew, and his mother, from an old New York Presbyterian family, had given up religion when they were young, and that he himself had never been inside a church except for school field trips. He spoke skeptically about government and other institutions, including the college, whose restrictive rules he and all the upperclassmen he knew found oppressive and hypocritical. When Ben spoke, he often did not look at Stevie, but instead sent his words out into the empty air, as if he were addressing some invisible assemblage. Stevie watched him attentively, and he could not tell whether what he said impressed her or shocked her. In her presence, he learned that his own words could taste bitter even as he spoke them.

Each morning Ben would order himself to stay away from Stevie that day, but in the evening he usually sought her out. He had had girl friends before, in high school and college, but, he now thought, they had been so much like him that they might just as well have been his sisters. They were sarcastic and conceited, in training to replace their enervated, brittle mothers. Although Stevie was just as bright, she did not wield her intelligence like a weapon. She seemed direct and clear, like a child. And though her simplicity often made Ben uncomfortable, he loved her for it. It was almost as if he hoped she might redeem in him the very faults that she made him so conscious of.

Many evenings, they would have coffee at the college snack bar. There they would chat for an hour or so, and Ben's friends often joined them. Kathy Gauss, who played the dulcimer and swore like a truckdriver; Kodji, a taciturn Ugandan who was captain of the soccer team and who was said to receive monthly supplies of powdered rhinoceros horn from home; A. T. Taylor, a beatnik girl from Paoli who was having a sonnet cycle published in the spring; Jim Peterson, a tall, blond Swede from Minnesota, who, people whispered, would be *teaching* at the Institute for Advanced

Studies next year. One night, as he listened while Fergus Clancy, the congenial campus anarchist, dissected the Kennedy family, Ben caught Stevie staring at him, her eyes shining.

"Aren't you ever afraid that I'll fall in love with one of your beautiful geniuses?" she said after Fergus had left.

"I guess I hope they'll help you fall in love with me," Ben said.

"You don't need any help," Stevie said, her eyes lowered.

"What?" Ben said. Then he blushed, because of both the sudden new intimacy itself and his obtuse reaction to it. "I couldn't believe . . . Listen, I am in love with you too. I think . . . I was surprised . . ."

Stevie looked up. "Well," she said, her eyes dancing, "*that's* settled, anyway."

Later that week Stevie started staying overnight in Ben's room. She was reluctant at first, because she was afraid of getting caught. When she finally agreed, Ben felt vaguely let down, he did not understand why.

Naked, they would lie together on his narrow bed. Cold autumn-night breezes from the slightly open window would brush over them, and at first they would shiver against each other, laughing quietly. Once together for a few minutes, they were warm, and they would touch each other, delighting in how finely made they were. He tried to tell her how he loved her, but he could not trust his words not to crack into foolishness. He would simply stare at her, astonished, and tears would sometimes sting his eyes. She would not permit him to enter her, and he was relieved that she would not—again he did not know why. They both had orgasms, though, sometimes simply from embracing. Then they would talk for hours, about other people on campus whom they liked or didn't like, about professors, about high school and home, and about themselves.

On Election Night, along with twenty or so other students, they watched the returns on a television set that Ben had set up in his dorm's parlor. He had also procured a pint of scotch, and by the time Illinois finally fell to Kennedy, he and Stevie were a little drunk. Afterward, in Ben's room, Stevie tried half-heartedly to hold him away from her, but he was so funny ("Und chust how long haff ve had zis little problem mit zex?" he asked her, in a tyrannical analyst's voice) that she finally yielded. It was his first time, and as he penetrated her, he felt at the heart of his intoxication a sadness as sharp as a nettle.

A week later, Ben was standing with Jed on the porch of the main building. They were waiting for Stevie to have lunch with them after her twelve o'clock philosophy class. The weather had been gray for days, and now a strong wind blew out of the east, stripping away most of the leaves that remained on the tall oaks on the front campus and promising a cold, sullen rain.

"What are you going to do with Mackler?" Jed said.

"I don't know," Ben said. "I called another meeting for after lunch. Yesterday, Mackler swore he hadn't been cheating, but Professor Prentice says he saw his crib sheet."

"What do you think?" Jed said.

"Oh, guilty, no question. He was really squirming. Anyway, some girl who sat next to him in the exam is going to testify this afternoon. I think she's going to back up Prentice."

From the corner of his eye, Ben saw Stevie walking toward the steps leading up to the porch; he did not greet her.

"You going to expel him?" Jed said.

"The guy is basically O.K. My committee wants to fire him, but I think I can talk them out of it," Ben said. He cupped his hands around Jed's pipe while Jed tried to get it lit for the fifth or sixth time. The wind blew the match out. "Jesus, Jed, when are you going to give up this silly-ass pipe? Next thing you know, you'll start wearing corduroy jackets with leather patches on the elbows."

Jed lighted his pipe. "We've got a visitor," he said.

Stevie, from behind Ben, covered his eyes with her hands.

"You're late," Ben said.

"I'm sorry," Stevie said. "I was arguing with Ginny about the mind-body problem after class."

"Yeah, Ginny's got a problem in both areas," Jed said.

"I remember those arguments in Phil. I," Ben said. "What a bunch of garbage."

"Oh, I don't know," Stevie said. "The class was pretty exciting today."

"Exciting, shmexciting," Ben said. "First of all, no freshman—Ahh, forget it."

"Big-shot junior," Stevie said, putting her arm around Ben's waist. He acted oblivious of her touching him, and she took her arm away. "What's wrong?" she said.

"Nothing," Ben said. "It's cold out here. Let's go in and eat."

As he started walking toward the door, he caught the glance that passed between Jed and Stevie, and he saw Jed put both hands out, palms up, and shrug his shoulders. He learned that from me, Ben thought.

"We suspended Mackler for two weeks—until after vacation," Ben reported to Jed later that afternoon in the locker room, as they were dressing for practice. "The girl saw the crib sheet, too."

Jed turned away from the full-length mirror, in front of which he had been striking menacing-lineman poses. He nodded his head, and Ben pounded his shoulder pads into place with his fists.

"You won, then," Jed said seriously, sitting down on a bench to lace his shoes.

"Yeah, but it took some time. Prentice was furious because the guy lied, and he wanted to kick him out. But I gave them all some crap about ruining somebody's future for one mistake."

Jed finished with his shoes, and he and Ben walked through the soccer team's section of the locker room and out toward the practice fields. It was raining now, a drizzle as fine and silvery as needles.

"Don't you think you've been a little rough with Stevie lately?" Jed said as they started jogging to keep warm.

"I know, I know," Ben said. "Since last week—maybe we shouldn't have done it. Sometimes I feel this . . . contempt, or something."

"Well, whatever it is, you're showing it."

"She's pretty tough, in a funny kind of way."

"It's you I'm worried about."

"Oh, sure."

"I just think you're in some kind of trouble," Jed called after Ben, who had veered away from him, toward the soccer field.

Near the end of scrimmage against the junior varsity later on, Ben threw himself forward, about two feet above the ground and parallel to it, and headed the sodden ball toward the goal. He had angled it well, just beyond the goaltender's reach, and it skidded into the net. He lay in the mud uninjured but shaken; the center fullback, in trying to clear the ball, had barely missed kicking Ben full in the face.

In the dim light cast by the streetlamp outside his window, Ben could just see Stevie smiling at him, her face hovering above him like a moon.

"There," she said. "That ought to take some of the grouch out of you." She rolled onto her back.

"I haven't given you any trouble since Tuesday," Ben said.

"You haven't given me much fun, either. You just needed me to relax you a little." She paused. "Are you sure it's still a good idea for me to go home with you Thanksgiving?"

"Of course. Just don't try to say grace, or anything."

"Don't you look up all your old girl friends when you go home?"

"No. Why? Are you thinking about Rick, or whatever his name is?"

"I was just teasing."

"Maybe *you* don't want to go any more. Maybe you want to go skiing or spelunking, or something."

"No. I want to be with you."

Ben sat up on the edge of the bed and put his feet on the floor. "Did you ever make love with Rick?" He was surprised by his own question—as surprised as he would have been if a stranger had at that moment broken down the door to his room.

"What difference does it make?" Stevie said, folding her arms over her breasts.

"Did you?"

"It's not your business. It doesn't make any difference."

"It makes a *difference*," Ben said. Ben heard that his voice had now turned into a peculiar rasp.

"You are so smart; how can you be so stupid?"

"I just want to know."

"It doesn't matter what I did before. You are the most interesting boy I've ever met."

"You did, didn't you?"

"Yes. Once. The night before I left for college. We both knew that everything would be changing. It was just good-by."

Ben was silent. He stood up and turned and looked at Stevie. Her arms still covered her breasts, and when she saw him looking at her, she drew her knees up. He thought of her lying with someone else, and he felt physically sick.

"Good-by!" he said finally. "It's not like kissing someone on the cheek, you know. You don't use it to say good-by with. Except *you* do. You would."

"Oh, Benny, stop."

"God! You're so naïve. You really mean that stuff about saying good-by. Nothing has any . . . dimensions with you. Everything is only what it is. You don't see any edges, any shadows."

"What do you mean?"

"Listen, you'd better leave." He felt as if he might faint.

Stevie stood up and dressed. He expected her to cry, but she didn't. She left without saying a word.

Toward dawn, after hours of wakefulness, Ben fell into a short, fitful sleep. He dreamed that he was conversing pleasantly with Stevie before a huge plate-glass window in the drawing room of an elegant house. Suddenly, he knew, without knowing how he knew, that a fire had started upstairs, in one of the house's many bedrooms. The fire spread to other bedrooms, but still no smoke or heat was perceptible downstairs in the room where he and Stevie were talking. Stevie seemed completely unaware of the danger they were in. Ben tried to continue the conversation, to avoid alarming her, but his apprehension grew within him, like the fire itself. Finally, the acrid smell of smoke reached him, and he realized that the fire now threatened to consume the entire structure. Without a word, he threw himself forward, shattering the window into thousands of silvery needles of glass, and landed unhurt on the hard, frozen ground outside.

The morning was brilliant but frigid, a hard edge of deep winter protruding backward into November. Ben was in front of Stevie's dormitory at eight forty-five. As he entered the lobby, the dizziness he had felt the night before returned, blurring his vision. He called Stevie's hall on the lobby phone, and asked the girl who answered if Stevie was there. After a minute or so, Ginny, Stevie's roommate, came through the door that separated the lobby from the rest of the dormitory. She walked over to where Ben stood.

"She doesn't want to see you," Ginny said. "She is devastated."

"'Devastated,'" Ben said.

"Yes, devastated, Mister Sarcasm," Ginny said, tossing her short, mousy hair indignantly. Ben had a vision of this unattractive, theatrical girl carrying emotional freight from one person to another for the rest of her life.

"I'll wait for her," Ben said.

"She says you must leave her alone," Ginny said. Ben heard an echo of Stevie's firmness in these words. "And in my personal opinion," Ginny said, lapsing back into melodrama, "you are a son of a bitch."

Ben looked at the dead receiver, which he was still holding. He did not hang up but put the receiver down beside the phone and went out into the cold, bright air.

He walked to the library. He meant to try to study, but instead he sat down, bewildered, on the steps that led up to the building's entrance. After a while, he saw Jed coming toward him. Look at the way he walks, Ben thought—like some kind of cowboy. He felt a sudden surge of affection for his friend.

"You look terrible," Jed said when he reached the steps. "Why are you sitting out here?"

Ben stood up. "Because I've read everything in there," he said, his voice breaking. He rested one arm on Jed's shoulder and bowed his head. "You were right," he said, now crying. "I am in trouble."

Reunion

There was something about the sound of a pedal steel guitar that made Dave almost want to weep. It was so pure and liquid, nearly unearthly. He turned the car radio up and listened intently to the high, keening harmony of the pedal steel as it wove its way around the woman's plaintive voice:

> "If I could again be a little girl.
> Then I wouldn't be lonesome,
> And I wouldn't be hurtin',
> And I wouldn't be cryin'
> Over a big boy like yew."

Dave and Anne were on the way from New York to Swarthmore College, near Philadelphia, for Dave's tenth reunion. Dave reflected that he never felt so at peace as he did when he was on a car trip, suspended between two obligations, hurtling along with thousands of other anonymities, inaccessible to the world at large.

Anne leaned forward, turned the radio off, and began slowly striking the dashboard with her closed fist: Thump thump thump. Thump thump thump.

"I can't play when I'm driving, especially at night," Dave said.

"Come on, Davey. It's the only time I can beat you," Anne said, still thumping.

"You damn straight it is."

"Well, come on," Anne said, and started to emphasize the third beat: Thump thump *thump*. Thump thump *thump*. "You start."

Thump thump "Olympia," Dave said, over the third beat.

Thump thump "Augusta," Anne said. "Augusta" started with the last letter of "Olympia." That was the point of the game.

Thump thump "Atchison."

Thump thump "Nanking."

Thump thump "Gronsk."

"Gronsk! Gronsk!" Anne laughed and sat back.

"Yeah, Gronsk. It's a small mining town in the southwest Ukraine. Beria was born there, if I remember right. So I win. The score stands one nothing."

"Bullshit," Anne said.

"Ah, well, if you insist on being a filthy, vile cheater like the rest of your pinhead family."

"You couldn't think of anything so you made up a name and I *win*."

"Remember on the Vineyard last summer when I caught your mother moving her croquet ball? Jesus! What is she— over seventy? Came all the way from Omaha to move her croquet ball on Martha's Vineyard."

"I got the weirdest letter from her today. Did I tell you?"

"Your brother Topper cheats at Monopoly and your other brother, Peter, calls aces faults in tennis," David said, and smiled, as if pleased with having discovered a pattern.

"As I was saying," Anne said, "my mother wrote this nice long letter. It was on Brown Palace Hotel stationery. Did I tell you that she hasn't bought stationery in ten years?"

"So what was so weird?"

"At the very end, she said, 'If I were you, I'd slap David right across the face.'"

"Oh, *that's* cute."

"She didn't explain it at all. Just wrote it down out of the blue. I think she thinks I want to get married and you don't."

"The Brown Palace Hotel?" David said.

"Maybe we should get married, Davey."

"I thought you didn't want to."

"The Brown Palace is a hotel in Denver, and I don't know what I want."

They left the Jersey Turnpike at Exit 3, drove a few miles,

and crossed the Delaware River on the Walt Whitman Bridge. Over the bridge, on the Industrial Highway, they went by a small section of shabby row houses, a wilted outgrowth of residential Philadelphia sitting in the midst of truck routes and oil refineries. Whenever Dave had passed this place on his way to or from Swarthmore, he had had a strong desire to pull off the highway and take up life in one of those houses. He felt the lure even more strongly now, ten years later.

"You're daydreaming about trailer parks again, aren't you?" Anne said.

"We could have six or seven children with weak enamel like mine, and we could go blotchy, and I could run a concession at the stadium. It's almost walking distance. I'd get to see all the Phillies and Eagles games. Mike Schmidt and I would grow old together."

"You have no idea how upset your low-class urges make me," Anne said.

"I don't want to go in. Should we go in?" Dave said as he and Anne leaned over and peered down through a ground-level window into the murky beer cellar of the Swarthmore Student Center. They had parked near the center, which used to be the library when Dave was in college, and had then circled around it on foot a few times, Dave getting more and more anxious.

"It's your reunion," Anne said.

"I can't make out who's in there. Oh, Jesus; that's Leo Kriptich. He was president of the outing club. And there's Marge Simpson. Listen, let's walk around for a while. It's only nine o'clock."

The campus seemed Eden-like under the soft mid-June sky. The seniors had graduated the Sunday before, and the buildings and vast front lawn were quiet and empty except for a few ghostly, furtive-looking alumni. As they walked, Dave recounted stories associated with each landmark: Terry Hallowell getting drunk one night near graduation and putting his fist through the glass panels of all the lamp-posts on Magill Walk leading up to Parrish, the college's main building; the single week one spring when eight girls on the same hall in Willets dormitory feared they were pregnant; Folk Festival in his junior year, when he emceed the Doc Watson-Jack Elliot concert in Clothier Hall and was so nervous onstage as he made the introductions that he repeatedly and rapidly tugged at and released his Speidel Expandable watchband, much to the amusement of his friends sitting in the first few rows.

In front of the student center once again, Dave said, "Let's just make believe we're not doing this," took Anne by the arm, climbed up the marble steps, and walked through the door. "Uh, ha-ha, alumni, '64, you know," Dave said to the college guard sitting at a desk in the lobby. "I know," the guard said, and pointed toward the stairway that led down to the basement.

"Listen, I was sort of a leader back then, so a lot of people may, you know, come up to me and everything," he whispered to Anne just before they entered the cavernous tap-room.

"I know," Anne whispered back. "That's why I'm so hopelessly obsessed with you every night and day."

Down the middle of the room, about ten knots of seven or eight people were strung out like an archipelago. Most of them looked at the door to see who was coming in, and when they saw Dave, a good number rushed over to greet him. Dave shook hands with everyone and introduced Anne to the people whose names he remembered. Many lingered near the newcomers, forming a ragged circle around them as if they were the last two survivors of a game of dodge ball or were expected to provide some kind of entertainment.

"No, no; we're not married," Dave said. "No, no children, either," he said to someone else, who hadn't heard the first question. "I *hope*," Dave added, and laughed. "None that I *know* of, anyway." Anne jabbed him in the ribs. "Oh, I'm doing a little teaching at Columbia." . . . "Journalism." . . . "Yeah. Drove down from New York just now." . . . "No, thanks; we're staying with some friends of my parents over in Media."

They checked in at the Media Inn Motel a couple of hours later. "Don't you just *adore* motels?" Anne said when they got inside their room. She turned the TV on. Johnny

Carson appeared, looking as pink as a Spaldeen. "No *Arizona Highways*," she complained, after looking through the magazines. "No Massage-A-Bed."

They both stripped down to their underwear and lay down on the bed. Carson was finishing up his monologue. "Our staff secretary, Gloria Mishkin, is so friendly she's the only girl who ever received a team ball from the Los Angeles Rams," he said. "But now she's thinking about getting married. The only trouble is—"

"You know, all the men really looked at you tonight," Dave said, admiring Anne's figure.

"Everyone I talked to had children," Anne said.

"One point six," Dave said.

"You certainly were a free spirit back then," Carson was saying to his first guest, Adrienne Barbeau, the actress who plays the daughter on the TV show "Maude."

"This fellow had me convinced that he was Philip Roth," Adrienne Barbeau said.

"God, that tall guy was impossible," Anne said. "He talked to me for half an hour about what the suffixes on his American Express card meant."

"So one day I went to the library and got a Philip Roth novel and looked on the back of the dust jacket," Adrienne Barbeau said.

"Yeah, Eddie always was a bore," Dave said. "In college he was always talking about his courses and papers and stuff. He thought you were supposed to, or something." Dave got up and went into the bathroom.

"So you fell for the old Philip Roth trick," Johnny Carson said.

"It all makes me feel so old," Anne said.

"Old schmold," Dave shouted from the bathroom. "They're old, not you." He came back and stood over the bed with nothing on but an inch-wide loop of paper around his waist on which was printed "SANITIZED . . . FOR YOUR PROTECTION."

"Oh, you're so romantic," Anne said, holding out her arms.

"We'll be right back after this break," Johnny Carson said.

They slept until eleven Sunday morning, when the chambermaid knocked on their door. They drove five miles north on the Baltimore Pike, to a pancake house for breakfast. The place was filled with lower-middle-class suburban families, and many of the tables, Dave noticed, accommodated six or seven people. He and Anne were seated at a table for four. "Ninety-nine different breakfast combinations," Dave murmured from behind the outsize menu. "The El Ranchero looks pretty good, but so does the Clint Eastwood. What are you going to have?"

"The Phoenix Phrench Toast," Anne said. They gave their

orders to the waitress, who asked them if they wanted "creamery butter or fresh margarine."

After breakfast, they drove back south on the Pike about three miles and turned east on Route 320, the road into Swarthmore. They arrived at the college just before one o'clock and the beginning of the Alumni Day Parade of Classes. The sun shone brightly, and the stately front campus, divided by Magill Walk and its long, flanking procession of huge oaks, looked even more beautiful than Dave had remembered.

Dave didn't want to march with his classmates, so he and Anne stood on the porch of Parrish to watch the parade. A college maintenance truck was parked on the lawn near the walk that passes in front of Parrish, and in the truck's van, a band, composed of faculty members and townspeople, was warming up.

"Welcome to Alumni Day 1974," said a man standing at a microphone in the truck. "Let's start off with a big welcome for the class of 1904!" Out of the confusion in front of the main building's west wing, six very old people emerged —four women and two men. The band struck up "When the Saints Go Marching In," and the ancient alumni, most using canes and one old man being pushed in a wheelchair, hobbled and limped along the walk. "Aren't they wonderful!" the man at the microphone said. Next came the class of 1909, whose contingent consisted of two cheerful-looking old women. Then the class of 1914, whose representatives numbered twelve, a few of them in apparently fine health. The band played "Over There."

Each succeeding group was larger and more robust than its predecessor, and the music picked up in tempo and brightness as the parade went on. The class of 1929 was accompanied by what appeared to be some of their grandchildren. The band played "The Charleston Rag," and the small children ran and danced in and out of the ranks of the marchers. The class of 1949, observing their twenty-fifth reunion, was the largest, and they were led by a shiny yellow 1949 Hudson convertible. The men were sleek and prosperous-looking, and the women were dressed fashionably.

The size of the contingents now began to dwindle, though Dave's class seemed unusually numerous. There were only fifteen from the class of 1969, and four or five self-conscious and freaky kids from the class of 1972 brought up the rear.

For a moment after the parade ended, Dave felt death everywhere—in the trees, in the people, in the buildings, in the very sunlight that was ripening everything around him.

Since they had just eaten, Dave and Anne decided not to go to the alumni lunch. A tenth-reunion buffet was to be held late that afternoon at the house of the college's vice-president, Henry Freund, whose son Twigs had been a classmate of Dave's. But there was nothing in particular to do in the intervening time, so Dave and Anne found themselves at loose ends.

They walked down into the Crum, a fifteen-acre meadow lying southeast of Swarthmore's main campus. A narrow creek flows along one of the meadow's edges, and in the fall and spring it had been a favorite place for parties and rendezvous when Dave was in school.

"Susie Quinn and I used to come here all the time when I was a junior and senior," Dave said. "She never liked it—tripping over other couples, watching out for the campus police. I never really got anywhere with her.

"We used to sing a song about this place:

> Crum Creek is a coed's doom,
> Murmuring voices fill the gloom.
> Then there comes a sudden hush—
> Broder searching underbrush.
>
> Yea, morals matter;
> Yea, morals matter;
> Yea, morals matter;
> No sin at old Swarthmore,"

Dave sang, to the tune of "Yes, Jesus Loves Me." "James Broder was dean of men when I was here. He expelled people for holding hands and everything."

"Why didn't you get anywhere with her?" Anne asked.

"She was from the South. Also she was scared to death of getting pregnant. Nobody took the Pill."

They had circled the meadow and were walking up the road that led back to Parrish. "Listen," Dave said, "a friend of mine got his girl friend pregnant because they both believed that she couldn't get pregnant unless she had an orgasm. That is a true story." He paused for a moment. "It was only *at that time* I didn't get anywhere with Susie, I should add."

"What a pleasure to see you . . . David," President Amory said, meeting them as they walked out of the new library. He had hesitated over Dave's name for a second, but then found it and snatched it up as if it had been his misplaced wallet. "And this must be your wife."

"No, President Amory, this is Anne Springer, a friend," Dave said. "Anne, this is President Amory of Swarthmore."

"How do you do, Miss Springer. How are you, David?"

"Good," Dave said.

"Good," President Amory said.

"Well, we're just down for the reunion," Dave said.

"Fifth, isn't it?"

"Thanks, but it's the tenth."

"That isn't possible. Simply isn't possible. It seems like just last week you were scoring one goal after another on the soccer field." Dave blushed. "Just here for the weekend?"

"We drove down from New York last night," Dave said.

"You must come and visit me and Mrs. Amory sometime."

"Yes, just for the weekend," Dave said. "In fact, we may be leaving tonight."

"So: you're still a carefree bachelor, eh, David? We must do something about that, don't you think, Miss Springer? Ha ha. Nice to see you both," President Amory said, and went into the library.

Dave and Anne stood in the corner of the large flagstone terrace behind Vice-President Freund's house, along with eighty or so other '64s and their wives or husbands. The house sat on a hill opposite the college, and from the terrace there was a broad view of woods, the meadow, and the main campus beyond. Yellow light from the evening sun brought every tower, tree, and open space into a single harmony. Dave felt a yearning to be frozen into the panorama before him, to be down there next to the giant sycamore casting his own, small murky-blue shadow.

Supper was served buffet style. Anne ate lots, but Dave said he wasn't hungry and had another drink instead. Then Anne met a girl, the wife of a '64, who had been in the class ahead of her at Smith, and Dave drifted off by himself. The outdoor lights shone down on the center of the terrace, and for a moment Dave saw them as spotlights, and the people beneath as performers. They appeared to be speaking, gesturing, changing positions as if coached.

From the middle of the circle of light, a pretty blond girl glanced at Dave and seemed to recognize him. She said a few words to the tall man she was with, and, smiling broadly, detached herself from him and made her way through the milling, animated group to where Dave was standing alone.

"Aren't you Dave Schreiber?" she asked.

"Yes, and you're Amy Stahl."

"Amy Stahl Neuman, now," she said, nodding in the direction of the tall man.

"As of when?"

"A couple of years ago."

"You waited a long time," Dave said.

"Are you married?" Amy said.

"No."

"Forgive me, but I'm a little high. I was always curious about you in school," she said, lowering her eyes.

"Don't worry. I'm high, too. Why did you wait so long to get married?"

"I was teaching retarded children, and I told myself that I was too wrapped up in my work."

"But?"

"But—I don't know. I didn't think anyone was good enough, or—I really don't know."

"And why were you curious about me?"

"I guess I thought you were scary," Amy said.

"Scary. I thought you were incredibly *clean*," Dave said, and threw some of the ice from his glass across the lawn. "You were a cheerleader."

"And beneath your contempt."

"On the contrary, I had a long-distance crush on you from the time we were freshmen." Dave put an ice cube into his mouth.

"You never spoke more than two words to me in the whole four years."

"I was afraid to," Dave said, and chewed the ice into frozen fragments.

"I would have fainted if you had asked me for a date," Amy said, laughing.

"So what do you think now?"

"Of what?"

"Of my scariness."

"You seem very nice, but a little fed up," Amy said.

"You don't."

"No, I can honestly say I love my life—my husband, my son, everything," she said, making a broad sweeping movement with her right hand which looked to Dave like a high-school-play gesture.

"I don't know if I believe you," he said.

"Maybe *that's* why I was afraid of you."

Anne wanted to drive back, but Dave insisted that he was all right. The Saturday-night traffic was light, and he said he felt quite sober. Nevertheless, when they got to the Lincoln Tunnel toll plaza, he pulled out from the end of a line of six or seven cars and sped toward an open booth, not realizing that another car was approaching the same booth on a straight course. The front end of Dave's car hit the side of the other car. One of Dave's headlights was shattered and the other car had slight body damage, but nobody was hurt.

Friends and Relations

After about a half an hour of making out reports, the policeman who handled the accident, and who kept calling Dave "David," sent them on with repeated, stern admonitions to Dave to get the light fixed immediately. In Manhattan, Dave drove downtown and then through the busy, garish Village streets, feeling like an old man with a cataract.

Voices

Cassie's function was to check facts. She worked for a national news magazine, on the forty-seventh floor of a concrete-and-steel office building on Sixth Avenue. A reporter would write a story and give Cassie the material—newspaper articles, interview notes, press releases—on which the story was based. Cassie then measured the facts in the story against the source. When she came across a mythological allusion ("The President was at Camp David last weekend, brooding about his most recent difficulties like Achilles in his tent") or a random piece of general information ("Freud said that every dream was the fulfillment of a wish, but scientists now believe . . ."), she left her windowless cubicle and walked down the hall to the magazine's windowless library. There she looked up the reference and checked its accuracy. If, for one reason or another, there was no written source, or not enough time to look things up, Cassie could telephone people who could check facts for her. The Bronx Botanical Garden people knew about plant taxonomy. The people at the British Information Service knew about England. The scientists at the Manned Space-craft Center in Houston knew about the moon.

Whenever she found a mistake, Cassie drew a little balloon in the manuscript's margin and wrote inside it what change should be made. When she or a fellow checker allowed a mistake to get into the magazine, it was pointed out on a tally sheet posted each week on a bulletin board outside the library. During her first month of checking, Cassie made two errors. In a review of a new book about Virginia Woolf's last years, Cassie failed to correct "Miss Woolf" to "Mrs. Woolf." And in an article about an increase in urban crime, she let 42.6 per cent go through as 4.26 per cent. In both cases, readers wrote to the magazine. And in both cases, Cassie's name went up, alongside her mistake, on the bulletin-board tally sheet. She felt humiliated by these lapses and their promulgation, like a schoolgirl who has written a poor essay and who has then had to listen while the teacher reads it to the rest of the class.

After the first month, Cassie grew increasingly careful in her checking. Every fragmentary assertion of fact was an enemy until she brought it under control by verifying or correcting it. After four or five more months, she stopped looking at the tally sheet; she knew her name wouldn't be there any more. The editors and reporters found her work sometimes legalistic ("Kans. *not* geog. center of U.S. since admission of Alaska and Hawaii," she wrote in one tiny balloon) but otherwise impeccable. She had decided to make no more mistakes.

Cassie was from the Midwest, and she had visited New York only once before she went to work there. During her senior year in college, she had come East for an interview with the magazine. The personnel man had admired her zeal. "I want to be a journalist because I want to be involved with helping people know the truth," she had written in her letter asking for work. During the interview, he had found her perhaps a little too anxious to please. She had nodded her head vehemently in agreement with practically everything he said. "I can't deny it," she would say, her head bobbing like one of those toy animals that have flexible springs for necks. "That's for certain; no question about it." But the personnel man had realized that she was bright and would work hard, so he offered her a checking job starting immediately after she graduated.

After staying in a midtown hotel for a week, Cassie rented an apartment in the Village. She could have found something larger and sunnier for the same price, but this one was close to the subway she took to work. Also, she liked its split-level effect. You stepped into the apartment on a sort of balcony about five feet wide. Four steps directly opposite the front door led down into the rest of the room. Except for where the steps were, the balcony was separated from the sunken part of the room by a curious wrought-iron railing about three feet high. Cassie called it "the guard rail" to herself. The kitchen and bathroom lay to the left of the main room, off a short, narrow hallway, which was actually an extension of the balcony. There was a large window at the far end of the main room. So little light came through it, however, that it was more like part of the wall than a window.

Cassie kept her place neat and rather bare. She hung a few geometric prints on the walls, and got a handsome blue Rya rug for the floor. She used a studio couch for both sofa and bed, and put the old TV set that she had bought at a pawnshop opposite the couch, in front of the boarded-up fireplace.

George Austen, the reporter who had written the article about crime which Cassie had checked and made a mistake on, came to see her the day the mistake was posted. "Don't worry about it, keed," he said. "The only people who make mistakes are the ones who breathe." He asked her if she wanted to go to the New York–Milwaukee game with him that night. She didn't know what sort of game he was talking about, but she felt that she should oblige him because of the error. "That would be nice," she said.

She had never seen anything like Madison Square Garden before. As they stepped from the ramp onto the tier of the arena itself, the vastness of the enclosure made her dizzy. The game had already started, and the spectators' din was cascading down onto the brightly lit court as if it were the narrow end of a funnel.

Cassie knew very little about basketball. She barely heard George's explanations, though he put his mouth very close to her ear and shouted. She could not stop staring around the stands. Everywhere she looked, she saw the flares of matches or cigarette lighters, like pinpoint signals from one shore to another. On the court, huge black men ran up and down like frantic children walled in by darkness. During the second half of the game, George gave himself over to the frenzy of the crowd. He groaned and whistled and stamped his feet. He shouted things that to Cassie sounded like gibberish. "Back door again!" "Oh, no! Dollar bill's got five!" Late in the game, something brought the crowd to their feet in a deafening explosion of noise. As George sat down, he turned to Cassie. "The Pearl is beautiful!" he yelled with tears in his eyes.

Later, at dinner, the assurance that George had in the office and at the game melted away. He was twitchy and moody. Cassie thought she saw him slip a pill into his mouth. He talked sporadically about the magazine—the reactionary editorials, the men he hated, the way they butchered his writing. "That rag has as much to do with the world as a novel," he said. Cassie nodded in agreement, though she knew few of the people he mentioned. Every now and then, after another tirade or an awkward silence, George would seem to remember that he was on a date and would ask Cassie something about herself. Uncertain about what was expected of her, Cassie answered these questions briefly but with great eagerness.

In front of the door to Cassie's apartment, George asked if he could come in for a while. Cassie said would he mind if she said no this time; she felt very tired. He then tried to kiss her, but she turned her head slightly so that he kissed her cheek. He held her for a second or two and cursorily pressed against her. When Cassie got inside, she realized that she had been having a severe headache.

For a while, Cassie went out with Paul Dunbar, one of the magazine's five senior editors. He was a tall, handsome man, married to an alcoholic wife. He usually took Cassie to dinner or an early movie, and sent her home in a cab. For the most part, Cassie found it easy to be his companion. He carried most of the conversation, speaking in a bluff, stagy voice and twisting one end of his blond mustache. He talked mostly about the South, where he had been born and raised, and about how awful New York was. Cassie sometimes tried to bring up her own childhood. Paul would listen politely and interject a lot of "mmmms." But these symbols of attention were usually off in their timing, and when Cassie was through, she felt as if her words were lying around her like refuse.

Paul took her to his apartment one night when his wife was away. He muttered and groaned while making love to Cassie. He sank almost immediately into a deep sleep, but she could not sleep the whole night. She tried to hear what Paul mumbled when he turned over or changed position. After that night, he never asked her out again. She couldn't decide whether she felt angry or relieved.

Cassie had a brief friendship with Karen, another checker, who worked in one of the cubicles next to hers. When Karen got in in the morning, she would knock on the wall to say good morning, and Cassie would knock back. Later, Karen would stop by Cassie's desk and make arrangements to meet at the snack bar in the basement for lunch. She always had errands to run. She would then turn up ten or fifteen minutes late, offering a clutch of packages and a shrug by way of apology. Karen's interests were clothes and men. She did not much like talking about checking. After a time, Cassie began to get angry about her friend's chronic lateness and vapid talk. When Cassie told her one day that she had decided to try to save money by eating lunch in her office, Karen looked surprised and hurt. This reaction gave Cassie a brief and unpleasant sense of power.

After about a year, Cassie had very little life outside of her job. Even her apartment, which had at first seemed to her a quiet haven, became less welcoming. A drunken woman and her two teen-age sons moved in upstairs, and many evenings they argued with each other in loud voices. "Who do you think you are!" Cassie would hear the mother shouting. "Don't you listen when I tell you . . ." She could not make out the rest. These arguments often lasted until late at night, and Cassie started having trouble sleeping. She wrote a letter to the building's landlord, but never received an answer. She began staying late at the office, taking on much more than her share of work. She also began double-checking facts that she already knew were O.K. but couldn't leave alone.

One Monday morning, a man named Dave Schreiber called Cassie up at work. He was a teacher at Columbia Journalism School, he said, and he was writing a free-lance article for the *Times* about what it was like to be a young single woman in New York. Cassie asked him how he had gotten her name. He wouldn't say, but she thought she remembered Karen's mentioning a name like his. She agreed to answer his questions over the phone. His voice was calm and professional, like a doctor's or a priest's, and Cassie had no reluctance about telling him of her life—even personal details. At the end of the interview, Schreiber said, "You don't sound to me like you'd mind having your real name used." "Oh, no," Cassie said, laughing. "I have nothing to hide." When she hung up, she neglected her work for a while, and tried to imagine what sort of face Schreiber might have.

The article appeared in the *Times* the next Monday. Cassie quickly found the part about her.

> Cassie Jennison typifies the plight of the young career girl from out of town whose work comes first. She lives by herself in a small but charming apartment in a Greenwich Village brownstone. An editorial researcher for Tempo magazine, Cassie usually stays at the office until 8 or 9 P.M. during the week and sometimes has to work on weekends. This kind of schedule leaves little time for socializing, and can often lead to a feeling of isolation.
>
> "The worst times come at night, after work," Cassie says, pushing her long dark hair away from her pretty but tired-looking face. "I turn on the television just to hear the sound of human voices." Asked about the men in her life, Cassie straightens some papers on her desk which don't need straightening. "I'm afraid there aren't any right now," she says with a nervous laugh. "Most of the New York men I've met don't really care about anything but their jobs or themselves. They never really listen to you."
>
> So for Cassie Jennison life in New York sometimes seems cold and empty. But she intends to stick it out, hoping to move up the ladder in her very competitive chosen field, journalism.

It seemed to Cassie as if she had turned toward a mirror to see how she looked and had found a stranger staring back at her. The facts and quotations were accurate (Karen might have told Schreiber about the mannerisms), but he had shaped them into a melodramatic caricature instead of a human being. Cassie felt almost physically diminished after reading the story, as if some obeah man had got hold of a hank of her hair and had been muttering incantations over it at midnight. She stuffed the newspaper into the wastebasket and tried to concentrate on her work.

That night, as she opened the door to her apartment, she heard the phone ringing. She walked hurriedly across the balcony and down the four steps to answer it.

"Hello there, Cassie Jennison. Barney here," a man said on the other end.

"I don't know any Barney," Cassie said.

"Barney read about you today in the paper. You sounded so lonely, Barney thought he'd call you from his little grotto just to have a chat."

"I'm sorry, but I'm not interested. I'm going to hang up now."

"Wait, baby. Barney thought we could have a little talk. Maybe we could get together and—" Cassie hung up, her hands trembling. Just before dawn that same night, she was violently awakened by a tremendous crash from the apartment above hers. The woman started yelling unintelligibly.

The next night at eleven o'clock, Cassie's phone rang again. She hesitated before picking up the receiver.

"Hello—Miss Jennison?" a deep male voice said.

"Yes," Cassie said.

"Miss Jennison, you don't know me, and I realize that making this call is very forward on my part, but—"

"Just leave me alone," Cassie said.

"No, just a minute, Miss Jennison. Please don't hang up."

He sounded respectable and well-educated; Cassie could not bring herself to hang up right away. After all, she said to herself, I don't know why he's calling. "Miss Jennison, I read about you in the *Times* yesterday, and I was very moved by the suffering you must have experienced on account of your isolation. My name is Roy Black, and I'm a businessman. I'm also single. I just wondered if there wasn't something I could do for you."

"It's nice of you to call, Mr. Black, but I'm perfectly all right. I can get along quite well on my own. Now good-by."

"Wait, Miss Jennison. Listen, I respect your independence, and believe me, this call is so unusual for me that I've been agonizing for two days now over whether to make it. Perhaps we could meet sometime, have lunch or a drink."

"I'm sorry, I must go now," Cassie said.

"If you won't meet me, maybe you could tell me just one thing I'm curious about." He hesitated, as if to make sure that Cassie was still on the phone. When he resumed, his voice sounded richer, and the words were somewhat slurred. "Just tell me, do you have nice large breasts? Are you touching them now?" Cassie was paralyzed for a second. Then she threw the receiver on the floor and began crying. She could still hear the man talking in a tinny, squawky voice, like a television-cartoon animal.

Cassie asked Karen to have dinner with her the next evening, Wednesday, so that she wouldn't have to go home. Karen said she had something else to do, some shopping, but

Cassie was very anxious, so she finally agreed. At the restaurant, Cassie told all about the phone calls and how afraid she was to go home. She hoped that Karen might invite her to stay over for a few days. But Karen treated the whole thing as some sort of gruesome joke; she seemed more amused than horrified by Cassie's experiences, as if they were something that had happened to someone in a book or in a movie. Cassie almost asked directly to be taken in for a time, but she could not. She drank a good deal of wine.

When she got home, she found two letters in her mailbox. She went upstairs and read them in her apartment, after taking the phone off the hook. One letter was written in neat, childish printing on onionskin.

> Dear Ms. Jennison,
> I read about you in the New York *Times* newspaper today (4/1/74). Like you, I often feel myself lonely, even though I live and study amongst thousands at this great university. In the article, I believe that I detected the cry of one human being in the wilderness calling out to another. If your present circumstance admits of the possibility of correspondence, with an eventual prospect of rendezvous, I am fascinated. Please do not allow any understandable inhibition to prohibit you from responding if you would like to.
>
> > Sincerely yours,
> >
> > Prabandar Chatterjee
> > Student of Nutrition
> > Pennsylvania University

The other letter was scrawled in leaky ball-point. The words were jaggedly and irregularly formed, like an unhealthy electrocardiogram, and after two or three letters they often degenerated into wavy lines. Cassie deciphered enough to learn that the man who wrote the letter was fifty-three and lived and worked in Brooklyn. Many of the sentences started with more or less readable disavowals, like "I know we could never be compatable" and "My age is a definite negative facter," and then became illegible. She was too exhausted from tension and sleeplessness to read the rest. She turned off the lights and lay down on the bed without undressing, hoping that the bleariness caused by the wine would make her sleep.

Three hours later, she jerked the upper half of her body up on her elbows and saw a man in her apartment, on the balcony. He was walking silently back and forth behind the guard rail. Cassie could not see what the man looked like, but she could see that his mouth was moving and that he kept his face turned toward her as he walked. She knew that when he realized there were steps leading down into the rest of the room—that the guard rail was not unbroken—he would come down toward her. She also knew she would then be able to hear what he was saying, and she dreaded that above everything else.

The man glided along the rail as if he were on some sort of track. At last, he paused by the stairs, looked down, and extended one foot toward the first step. When his foot touched the step, he vanished. It was then that Cassie knew she must scream for help.

He Takes No Notice

"Lie down on the bed, Davey," Elizabeth says. "I have a new game to show you." She has just come back from spending Christmas and New Year's with her parents down in Augusta. We do not live together, but she often stays at my apartment.

"I already like it," I say as I lie down.

"You old fool," she says. "It has nothing to do with that stuff." She walks over, stands at the head of the bed, and looks down at my face. "Now say something," she says.

"I don't know what to say," I say.

"Keep saying something," she says, laughing. "Say anything."

"I don't know what to say, I don't know what to say, I don't know what to say," I say. "Arma virumque cano," I say. "Get a bucket of chicken, have a barrel of fun."

The point, she explains to me after she stops laughing, is to look at the person who is lying down and make believe that his upper lip is his lower lip and vice versa. She then insists that we reverse positions so that I can share the joke.

"Are you ready, Peanut?" she says after she lies down. I tell her I am, and she recites a rhyme she remembers from her childhood.

> Catalina Madelina
> Hop Inside a Watermelon
> Hokum Spokum Soakum was his name,

it goes, or something like that. I have heard Elizabeth say it before, and have often asked her to repeat it slowly, but she never does.

"Did you see it?" she says.

"No."

"Then I'll do it again," she says. She does, and I stand there peering down at her like a prospector looking for gold in a pan. But I still can't "see it."

"You must have gnats in your eyes," she says. She stands up on the bed and gently bounces up and down on it, arms folded. She seems almost angry. Her brown eyes are blazing, as they say. This is just another example, I think, of how she gets over-emotional about small things.

I explain to her that I cannot see things as being upside down. For example, when they turn someone upside down on television—I mean, as an electronic sight gag—I still see him as a right-side-up person who happens to have been turned upside down.

"Now quit standing on the bed," I say. "You'll break it." She adds a few defiant bounces and gets down.

Over the next couple of months, this limitation of mine drives poor Elizabeth to a minor sort of distraction. She tries four or five more times to get me to laugh with her over the game. She becomes autocratic. She orders me to try it once more, like me when I am about to throw up my hands over the semi-moron in my freshman English class. She forces me to stand over her for as long as five minutes. She starts out with Catalina Madelina or some other hopeful chatter, but, usually, by the time she is finished, she is telling me that I must be crazy not to see it. Then, invariably, she gets up and stands on the bed and bounces, as she did the first time, annoyed at me beyond all proportion. She has learned that her standing on the bed will in turn make me angry. It seems that, having failed to make me laugh, she is willing to settle for making me angry. Each time, she bounces a little harder.

For my part, after a while I go through this ritual simply to oblige her. I stare down at her, my mind wandering as she babbles. I hardly hear her when she gears up from babble to complaint. How small and beautiful she is, I think, with her thick long hair. It is so dark brown as to seem almost black, with what a hairdresser would call auburn highlights. Sometimes I try to figure out why this game means so much to her. Or I think about how different we are, and I wonder what will happen to us.

Now it is the middle of March. The weather is awful. It looks as though the city has decided to cut back on springtime or dispense with it altogether. Perhaps the mayor does not believe that it constitutes an essential service. My students have been giving me one cold after another. Elizabeth's acting career appears doomed. Over the four years I've been seeing her, she has always seemed on the verge of getting a break. Now, however, it has been eight months since she had any work, except for the Listerine commercial she had made just before Christmas. It paid her pretty well, but she hates it, and not just because it's about bad breath. "It makes me look like a fireplug with nice hair," she says, and won't let me watch when it comes on.

Late one evening, I am grading compositions. This is the first year we have had scholarship kids from Harlem—"ghetto youngsters," our headmaster calls them, "our great new commitment"—at the fancy boys' school where I teach. In the desperate hope of getting something to read, I have assigned my juniors to write about racism in the school. I should have known better. All I have gotten is pious, ill-written junk. Except for this one white boy's paper, which I am reading now. "I find the Negroyd features rather repellant," he says, "with their thick lips, flat noses, and knappy hair."

"Try it once more," Elizabeth says from across the living room.

"I don't want to," I say.

She comes over and drags me out of the chair and into the bedroom. It doesn't work again, and she stands up on the bed.

"This is getting ridiculous," I say. "Somehow my ideas about adulthood never included spending half an evening hovering over some Cracker and the other half trying to fetch her down off a bed."

Elizabeth starts bouncing pretty vigorously.

"Come on, cut that out," I say.

Now she starts jumping. The wooden bed frame breaks, right in the middle of the side away from the wall, where one of the stubby legs is screwed in to the wood. The leg splays out and falls over, and the split frame vees downward to the floor.

"God damn it, I told you that was going to happen someday," I say. Elizabeth almost lost her balance when the frame broke, but now she stands straight, arms folded. I put my hands on her waist, in a polka grip, and half lift, half yank her off the bed. I raise my hands to her shoulders and shake her once—very hard, or so I think, because she loses her look of malevolence, puts one hand on the back of her neck, and turns her face to the side as tears start rolling out of her eyes.

"Jesus, I'm sorry," I say. "I didn't mean to hurt you. Are you O.K.?"

She says nothing. She puts her arms around me, her face still turned to the side, and starts to sob.

"Are you really hurt?" I say.

She nods her head yes. I hold her for a while as she cries. When she stops I pile some books up under the frame where it has broken, so that the bed is level again. I sit down on the edge to test it.

"Why is this game so important to you?" I say.

"It isn't," Elizabeth says. "It's just funny, and I can't believe how dumb you are."

"Where did you learn it?" I say.

"When I was home."

"Is this what people do in the South?" I say. "I mean, when they're not tuning up their cattle prods."

"This here is just one tiny island, you know," Elizabeth says. "You people up here think you know everything, just because you go around brooding all the time and know how to be sarcastic."

"Who taught it to you?" I say.

"That's n of your b," she says.

"Probably some boy named Darrel or Billy Jo," I say.

"It *was* a boy, smart-ass," she says. "His name is Carl, and he's a lawyer in my father's company."

"How did you happen to be lying on a bed in his presence, or vice versa?" I say.

"Oh, don't worry; we didn't do anything, if that's what you're thinking. He's just a nice guy. We had a couple of dates—that's all."

"Big toe, little toe. That's all I know," I say, quoting another of Elizabeth's rhymes. The truth is, I feel a few twinges of jealousy. I was once very jealous about Elizabeth. But now it seems to be wrong to be jealous, when I don't know where we are heading. So I keep my twinges to myself.

"Let's give up on the game," I say. "It only makes trouble."

In the middle of April, Elizabeth gets a letter from her mother, asking her to come down to Georgia again for a week or two. Her father has to have prostate surgery, and he wants Elizabeth to be there. "You know how your father feels," Elizabeth's mother writes. "He thinks you will be more comfort to him than your two sisters and I put together, and I believe the old fool may be right. He hasn't even gone to the hospital yet, and I already feel like I need a heart transplant myself (ha-ha)!!" Of course, Elizabeth goes.

I am glad when she leaves. The apartment seems bigger, and I go around burping loudly and frequently. In the street, I sometimes find myself doing the kind of internal self-dramatization that I used to practice in high school. "The young, handsome loner walks the streets of the cruel city seeking out danger and adventure in the underworld. Women nudge each other as he strides by, but he takes no notice."

Also while Elizabeth is away, I decide that I'm not going to teach any more after this year. It doesn't pay enough, and my plan of writing during summer vacations has not worked out. I am never going to be a writer, so I might as well leave teaching and work full time at something else. Maybe I can become an editor. I have mentioned the possibility of quitting to Elizabeth. She thinks it would be a mistake. She thinks I would miss teaching more than I realize. But now she is not here to talk me out of it.

I go to see Paul Swander, the school's headmaster, to tell him of my decision. He is a short, round, pale man, with skin that a novelist might say was like tallow. Lately, he has been even rounder than usual, and correspondingly shorter-looking, because he is in the midst of giving up a two-pack-a-day habit.

"Come in, David, come in," he says when he looks up from his desk and sees me in his doorway. "What can I do for you?"

I sit down across the desk from him and notice a slight tremor in his hands. I tell him that I will not be coming back the following September.

"This is a severe disappointment," he says. "I have come to think of you as one of our stalwarts."

I apologize for letting him down.

"Not two months ago, as I remember it," he says, "you told me that you would be returning to us next year. I mean, Christ . . ."

"That's true," I say, "but I have been doing a little re-evaluation."

"I thought that you shared the excitement over our new commitment to these ghetto youngsters." He pauses. For no apparent reason, I start thinking about how much Swander loves sports, and it suddenly occurs to me that the excitement that he feels about the ghetto youngsters may have more to do with his hopes for a league basketball championship than with anything else. "I guess promises don't mean as much to you young people as they do to my generation," he goes on. "This puts our personnel situation into a real bind. I mean, for Christ's sake—"

His phone rings, and while he talks my mind wanders again, but this time more usefully. "As long as we're on promises," I say after he hangs up, "perhaps you have forgotten the one you made to me three and a half years ago. You told me when I came here that when Mr. Little retired I could take over as chairman of the English Department." Not that I ever would have done it, I add, to myself. "Young though I would be, you said."

"You have something there," Swander says.

"Yet not two weeks ago, as I remember it, you sent the memo around announcing that Mr. Sib would be the new chairman next year."

"Well, you have a point there," Swander says. He looks hopefully at his telephone.

"Listen, Paul, let's don't either of us make a big deal over this," I say. "It's not exactly King Edward's abdication, is it?"

"But in any case we shall genuinely miss you, David," he says, hitting his stride once again. "You have made a genuine contribution here." Then he leans forward confidentially and says, "Ordinarily, this announcement is not made until moving-up day, but I think under the circumstances the seniors will forgive me if I tell you now that they have dedicated their yearbook to you and to our drama director, Mr. McGregor."

"I don't know what to say," I say. "I never would have guessed . . ."

"Oh, the boys have great respect for you, David."

I tell him how gratified I am, but I don't think I will be changing my mind. Then I go through saying how much I've profited from my association with the school and all that.

Near midnight on the next Sunday, Elizabeth returns.

"How is your father's rig?" I ask her.

"If you mean the operation, it went fine," she says.

I tell her about quitting. She says I did it behind her back. I tell her not to worry about money right now, I don't mind using my savings for a while. She says money is not what she's worried about.

When we are undressing for bed, I notice some purplish marks on her neck. They look like small wine stains on linen. She gets under the covers and lies on her side facing the wall. I sit on the edge of the bed. "Did you make love with him?" I ask.

"Yes," Elizabeth says.

"I don't believe you," I say.

"Yes we did," she says.

"Are you in love with him?"

"We must have done it twenty times—at my parents' house, at his parents' house, in his car. We even lay down in a road somewhere once. What are you going to do about it?"

"Anything I do would appear to be ex post facto," I say. "Are you going to answer my question?" After a minute or so of silence, I get up and go and sit on the john until my stomach calms down a little. Then I go back and get into bed. Elizabeth is pretending to be asleep. When I slide over and try to put my arms around her, I find that she is trembling slightly. She reaches her hand back and pushes me away.

A week later, Elizabeth leaves for good. She has packed most of her things and shipped them ahead to her parents. She is taking the train. I pick her up at her apartment and go with her to Penn Station. We have been speaking to each other only when we had to decide such matters as who would keep records that we couldn't remember who bought in the first place. But before she gets on the train I ask her to keep in touch, to let me know what happens to her. She says she will and that I should do the same. I hand her her suitcase near the rear of the train, and she turns to get on board. Then she stops, puts the suitcase down, and turns around to face me. She reaches up like a tiny French general about to bestow the Croix de Guerre. I bend over and she puts her arms around my neck and hugs me. Then she picks up her suitcase and boards the train. I walk along the platform as she walks forward through the cars. When she finds her sleeping compartment, she sits down near the window. I stand on the platform and try to pantomime things to her, or see if she can read my lips. I feel like Marcel Marceau. She laughs and shakes her head. Finally, partly because I think I ought to, I mouth "I love you" at her three or four times. She gets up, turns her back on the window, and walks into the corridor. The train starts, and I jog along with it for a hundred feet or so, but Elizabeth does not reappear.

Late in June, Elizabeth sends me an announcement of her wedding. I call her up, at her parents' home.

"Hello, Peanut," she says when she comes to the phone. My hand moves; I always put my hand on her shoulder when we greeted each other.

"Congratulations," I say. "You-all sure don't waste any time."

"You are so crass," she says. "Don't you know you're not supposed to congratulate the bride-to-be?"

"I don't know anything about that stuff," I say.

"Did you find your new job yet?" she says.

"I just finished all the end-of-the-year things for school, and I haven't really had time to look. Anyway, I feel exhausted. I keep waking up at five or six in the morning and then I can't get back to sleep."

"I have been worrying about you," she says.

"Oh, I'm O.K. If you were so worried, why did you leave with such alacrity?"

"I don't know what that means, but I wasn't happy to go, if that's what you're saying."

"Even with Darrel waiting for you in the road somewhere?"

"I was lying about all that," Elizabeth says. "None of that happened; I was just trying to get some kind of response from you. When you didn't seem to care, I had no reason to stay."

"But I *did* care," I say. "I just didn't think it was fair for me—"

"You think too damn much. You talk too damn much. Someday you're going to think so long about putting food in your stomach that you'll starve to death."

"That's not fair," I say. "I didn't know you were giving me some kind of emotional test, for Christ's sake."

"I wasn't giving you any test. I was just trying everything I could think of to find out whether you cared about me."

"Including leaving?"

"Including threatening to leave, which you did nothing to stop," she says.

"This all seems to be academic, in view of your impending nuptials," I say. "Are you going to have a honeymoon?"

"You know, when you shook me that time after I broke the bed, I wasn't hurt at all—not physically. And when I was on the train and you were jumping around outside the window like a drunken rooster, I was crying."

"Well, I couldn't see that," I say. "The glass was pretty dirty. All I could see was that you were smiling. And then you got up."

"Oh, what difference does it make," she says.

My mind wanders for a moment. "Listen," I say, "won't you please say 'Catalina Madelina' slowly, so that I can understand it?"

And she does.

Long Weekend

The Taconic Parkway is a four-lane highway, but the lanes are narrow and misanthropic, and in many stretches a low, murderous steel fence divides northbound from southbound. Dave was passing a lot of cars, and passing under these conditions, he told himself, took the nerve and judgment of a fighter pilot, a Blue Angel. Ordinarily, he enjoyed maneuvering up the Taconic, but the morning was so splendid that he resented the need to concentrate on driving.

"Did you sleep well last night?" Anne asked him.

"Not particularly," Dave replied. "I have the sense that this weekend is going to be a disaster."

"Listen, Ruth Masterman will be there. It's not like you won't know anybody."

"But I mean, who are these three guys? All young lawyers or accountants or something."

"Well, you met Bob Baron at my apartment," she said. "He's nice. You said you liked him, remember? He's the one who told about his father's collection of shirts."

"Shirts?"

"You remember. His father has hundreds of new shirts. He buys them and never wears them."

"Now I remember. Very little in the way of neck."

"You're too harsh, you really are. You *said* you liked him. Anyway, he's in analysis—five times a week."

"Well, that's a relief. It must make a big hole in his slimy income. Wait a minute, wait a minute: he lives in his father's apartment house, right? He has two bedrooms and pays twenty-seven dollars a month."

"That's right. And his father helped him rent this house we're going to. In fact, all three of the guys in on the house live in Bob's father's place. He knows a lot about real estate."

"And shirts."

They left the highway at the Millbrook exit. Anne began reading off directions that put them through a maze of back roads, the last of which was unpaved and wound up a steep hill. They passed ramshackle houses and estates that either looked completely abandoned or featured freaks tinkering with Hondas or simply lounging around. "What's this place supposed to be—'Deliverance'?" Dave said.

"It's about time," Bob said as he met Anne and Dave at the top of the driveway. He was a tall, hairy young man with a straight nose and thin lips. He was wearing tennis sneakers and shorts and no shirt. "We thought you two were going to chicken out."

"I was in my office until very late last night working on some course plans," Dave said. He wasn't. "I'm sorry. Anyway, didn't Ruth say that we might not be able to come Friday night?"

"Yeah, she said something about it. But we thought you two might not show at all."

"You already said that," Dave said. Anne stepped on his foot.

"Well, come on, you two. I'll take you to your room and then show you around."

The place had been a farm until about forty years ago, Bob explained. The farm had failed during the Depression, and a young New York City family had bought it to use as a country house. The couple had got divorced, but the woman kept the house and rented it, over the years, either to Bennett College students or to young professionals from the city. The owner was now in her seventies, Bob said, and knew his family very well.

The buildings and grounds were a shambles. The large main house, white with vestiges of green trim, badly needed painting, and the wood floors inside were warped and rippled. Bob and his friends had scattered their clothing and food and records all over the place, making it look like a college dormitory. The outbuildings, some of which were smothered by wild vines and creepers and barely visible, were falling apart. The big barn, behind the house, had gaping holes in it and seemed menacing. The clearance on its first floor was so low, Dave thought as he and Anne bent over to enter it, that it must have been built and worked by trolls. A jumble of ski equipment—poles, skis, and boots—stood against the wall to the left of the doorway. Down a slight incline, behind the barn, were a well-kept tennis court and one of those small raised-tank swimming pools with a spindly rail around it. The pool and court looked naked and anomalous.

Dave was rallying with Al Fleisch, one of the three shareholders in the house. Bob and the other renter, Jon Kline, had finished a match, and they and Anne and Ruth had gone over to the pool.

Al was quite fat, but he was surprisingly athletic. He had curly red hair and little eyes that seemed to be hiding out in his face. He had been learning tennis all winter, at a tennis club in the city, and though he was not nearly as good as his two housemates, he wasn't bad. Dave had played tennis ten or fifteen times in his life.

"Give it to him, Pork," Bob called from the pool. They started playing in earnest.

"Uphold the honor of the house," Jon yelled.

Al won the first two games easily. Then Dave began to get his flailing but powerful serve in. He also started to hit the ball more and more softly during rallies, with various slices and lobs. Every now and then, when the ball was coming to him just right, he would powder it with a forehand top spin, his one good orthodox shot. He won five games in a row, and Al was furious. He threw his racket against the high wire fence with increasing frequency and velocity. Dave ran all over the court picking up balls between points while Al steamed.

"I'm getting really lucky," Dave said apologetically as they changed sides for the eighth game.

"Ahh, I'm playing like some goddam girl," Al said.

"Come on, Pork, don't let a *guest* beat you," Bob shouted.

"You know, you're supposed to pick them up when you're at the net," Al grumbled, down 15–40, as he walked in to retrieve a ball.

"Christ, Al, I've been picking them up for you the whole time."

Dave won the set point and Al threw his racket over the fence, far back into some wild raspberry bushes.

"You let us down," Bob said when Dave and Al came over to the pool. "Got beat by a *guest.*"

"I was pretty lucky," Dave said.

"Yeah. You shouldn't run around your backhand so much," Al said.

The day grew very hot. Al spent the rest of the afternoon lying on and overflowing an air mattress in the center of the pool. When Dave went into the water, he had to swim around Al's edges. Jon and Bob sat at one end of the pool, playing ferocious backgammon, with their feet dangling in the water. They were playing for twenty-five dollars a game. Anne and Ruth sat talking at the other end. They were a novelist's dream of morphology: Ruth was slim and dark and flat, and Anne was fair-skinned, blond, and buxom—"busty," she called herself. Dave skirted the island, who was now fast asleep on his mattress, and poked his head over the edge of the pool in front of the two women.

"Where do you know these guys from?" he asked Ruth quietly.

"I only know Bob," she said. "I met him at work. He was with the city's corporation counsel for a while, and I saw him around City Hall."

"So do you love him, or what?"

"Oh, no. He's actually just an acquaintance, really."

"What does he do now?" Dave asked.

"He's with a big firm, I think. The city wasn't paying enough for him."

"By the way, I don't know if Ruth told you, but we usually charge our guests five dollars a day each—you know, for food and liquor and stuff," Bob told Dave as the whole group trooped back up to the house, late in the afternoon. "I hope that's O.K."

"Oh yeah, sure, fine," Dave said.

"Did you know that they're charging us ten dollars a day for this famous weekend?" Dave asked Anne in their room. They were changing for supper.

"No, Ruth didn't say anything about it. I thought it was free."

"Well, it's not. But I'll tell you one thing."

"What?"

"We better go out there and get to work on that Jack Daniel's."

The three hosts huddled around the outdoor charcoal grill arguing over hot dog and hamburger strategy. Dave and Ruth and Anne drank in the kitchen, while peeling and slicing potatoes and making a giant salad. Dave went to the refrigerator to get some butter. It was an old refrigerator—the kind with a small freezing compartment that has no door. Dave found the butter in the compartment, which was so roundly swollen with ice and frost that its original conformation was totally invisible. One small tunnel of space remained, just large enough for the stick of butter.

"Would you look at this?" he said. "They must have gone the whole year without defrosting. I couldn't live in a house with this on my conscience."

They ate supper outside, at a picnic table near the door to the kitchen.

The food wasn't very good. The hamburgers were almost raw, and the frankfurters were so charred they reminded Dave of Phillies' cheroots. Al nevertheless managed to eat a tremendous amount, claiming in between every two mouthfuls that he was following Dr. Atkins' diet very closely and that he had lost twenty pounds in the last month and a half. Everybody drank a lot of beer.

"Dave, I'd like to get your opinion on something," Bob said at the end of the meal. "You teach at Columbia Journalism, right? Well, have you seen those ridiculous ads on television for the *Daily News*? The ones where Truman Capote or Ayn Rand say how well written the *News* is?"

"Yes, I have," Dave said.

"I mean, someone like Capote is really selling out when he does something like that."

"What was it you wanted my opinion on?"

"Those ads are ridiculous."

"As a matter of fact, I think the *News* really *is* a well-written paper. It doesn't have much in the way of solid journalism, but what it does have is much better written than the *Times*, for instance."

"You can't say that!" Bob said. There was a silence at the table, broken only by Al's munching on the last ear of corn.

"That's right, you can't say that!" cried Jon in mock hysteria. He was a very short, intense young man with blond hair and slightly wild eyes. He had been drinking a great deal before supper and had started smoking marijuana just after he finished eating. He stood up at the table and began waving his arms around. "You can't say that!" he repeated. "I can say that, Anne can say that—anyone else can say that, but you can't say that." Everybody at the table laughed except Bob.

"I'm sorry. I guess I just didn't realize that I couldn't say that," Dave said, chuckling.

"That's all right," Jon shouted. "That's all right. Next time you want to say that, you just let me know and I'll say that for you."

On Sunday, Dave and Al played tennis again, and Dave won again. This time, however, there was no racket throwing or surliness on Al's part. Instead he affected indifference and nonchalance, refusing to try for shots that weren't close to him, staying on the base line, serving to the wrong court, and forgetting the score.

At the pool, afterward, Jon tried to persuade Anne and Ruth to take their bathing suits off. "Remember Ellen?" he said to Bob. "Now, there was a *guest*. She didn't wear hardly anything all weekend." Anne had become so self-conscious that she wouldn't even take off the shirt she wore over her bikini. "Listen, as long as we're back up here where the revenooers can't get at us, we might as well have a good time," Jon said, prancing around the edge of the pool.

"Honestly, Jon, why don't you try growing up?" Ruth said.

"It's you who aren't grown up. The human body is a glorious thing. Why are you ashamed? Here, we are living in a state of nature. Noble savages." He stopped in front of where Anne and Dave and Ruth were sitting. "I'm not ashamed," he said, and pulled down his swimming trunks.

"Jesus Christ!" Dave said. Anne blushed and turned away.

"Oh look! A Tijuana Small!" Ruth said.

"This is really incredible," Dave said to Anne later, when they were alone in their room. "It's like a cruel hoax of some sort. I really don't know if I can stand it till tomorrow."

Anne came over to the chair he was in and sat on his lap. "Listen, I know that what I'm going to say will upset you, but I have to tell you anyway," she said, putting her arm around his neck.

"What now?"

"Well, this morning Bob came in here to get some socks of his or something."

"It figures."

"Didn't you hear him?"

"No. I must have been asleep. A miracle."

"Well, I saw him. Anyway, Ruth told me at the pool today that before we got up, Bob was telling her and Al and Jon that you and I must not have a very good relationship."

"Oh, good," Dave said. "Where did he get that from?"

"He said we couldn't have a good relationship because we weren't sleeping holding each other."

"You must be joking."

"The only thing is that it really bothers me."

"It should bother you. Can you imagine the nerve of saying something like that!"

"No, I mean it bothers me that we don't sleep holding each other."

They left that evening, before supper. Dave made Anne give an excuse—something about having forgotten that she had promised to feed a neighbor's cats. "So, you're chickening out," Bob said at the top of the driveway.

"Well, you know," Dave said. "Listen, thanks a lot. We had a really good time." He handed Bob twenty dollars.

"Oh, look, you're not staying for supper; you don't have to pay the whole thing," Bob said, and handed back a five.

Sic Transit

"It wouldn't have happened in a Socialist system," Dave's father said as he backed the car down the driveway. He shifted around uncomfortably, compressing his lips and puffing out his cheeks the way he always did when he was tired or in pain.

"Maybe the driver just didn't see us," Anne said from the back seat.

"He saw us, he saw us," Dave said. "He doesn't like his job, and he decided not to stop for us—that's all."

Dave and Anne had spent Labor Day at Dave's parents' house in South Nyack. In the middle of the afternoon, they ate a big meal, which Dave's father cooked, grumbling as usual about having to get food ready at odd times of day. The idea had been for Dave and Anne to get an early bus, but for more than an hour after dinner Dave's mother went around the house and garden finding things for them to take back to the city. Anne followed her, squeaking gratefully as brown paper bags and shopping bags filled with books, potted begonias, cookies, clipped magazine articles, ears of corn, and cut flowers with their crushed stems wrapped first in a soaking-wet paper towel. The towel was in turn wrapped in a sheet of waxed paper, which was supposed to keep the towel from dripping but which Dave knew wouldn't. He trailed in the two women's wake, muttering about having to "carry all this crap to the subway, on the subway, and up the subway stairs." His father went to his room to lie down and rest his back.

Finally, Dave and Anne climbed the hill behind the house to Broadway and waited in the hot afternoon sun for the No. 9-A Red & Tan bus to New York. After a few minutes, the bus came into view a half mile north. It made its usual stops on the way toward the corner where Dave and Anne were waiting—where Dave had caught the bus hundreds of times in the past after visiting his parents. As it approached, Dave took a step into the road, set down the bags he was carrying, and waved the commuter tickets that his mother had pressed on him when she kissed him good-by. "Here comes the bus," he said. But instead of slowing down and stopping, the bus gathered speed. It charged past like a gigantic red bull, leaving Dave with his arm extended and the tickets in his hand flapping violently. The bus driver's expression was serene and remote, and the passengers stared curiously at Dave and Anne through the green-tinted windows as they went by.

"Did you see that?" Dave said. "That son of a bitch went right by. Did you see that?"

"It was pretty hard to miss," Anne said, stifling a laugh. "What'll we do?"

"The only thing is to get my father to drive us. We can get ahead of the bus because it doesn't go straight south. We can head it off at the Palisades light, where it turns onto Route 9-W. Son of a bitch."

"Why don't we wait for the next one?"

"Ahh, it'll be too crowded. Don't forget it's Labor Day, and it's getting late. If you and my mother hadn't spent all that time gathering freight, we—"

"Maybe we could go in in the morning. Your faculty meeting isn't till noon, is it?"

"I just want to get back," Dave said severely. He picked up the packages and walked quickly down the hill. Anne had to run to catch up to him.

"In a Socialist system, bus drivers wouldn't be exploited for the bosses' profit," Dave's father continued. They had left South Nyack and were driving toward Palisades on 9-W. He rather abruptly put his foot on the brake, for no discernible reason, and then mashed down on the accelerator. Something that sounded like marbles spilled out of one of the bags on the back seat when the brake went on, and then rushed eagerly under the seat when the car sped up.

"What was *that?*" Dave said.

"It's all right; calm down," Anne said, her voice muffled.

"Listen, in a Socialist system we probably wouldn't be riding along in this nice new Volvo," Dave said. There was a rustling of paper, and Dave turned around to see what was going on. Anne was down on all fours in the space between the front and rear seats, looking for whatever it was that had spilled. Dave reached back. "Teeckle teeckle," he said.

"Ppfff," his father said, leaning forward over the steering wheel.

As the bus slowly turned right onto 9-W, Dave walked out into the middle of the road, directly in the bus's path, and waved both his arms. He stayed there until it stopped completely and its door opened; then he and Anne got on. "You go back and find a seat," he told her after he had given the bus driver their tickets. "I've got a little business to attend to."

"Why didn't you stop for us in South Nyack?" he asked the driver.

"Just move out the way," the driver said. He was a short black man, not so much fat as he was round. He looked to Dave to be made out of spheres of flesh covered with taut, shiny skin.

"I asked you a question," Dave said.

"O.K., O.K.," the driver said, keeping his head facing forward. "Just move out the way so we can go."

"What are you talking about?" Dave said.

The driver pulled a lever, simultaneously closing the door and turning the post to which was attached a gate that swiveled out to separate the driver's area from the rest of the bus. The gate caught Dave in the stomach and gently forced him back into the aisle. The bus started rolling.

"Ain't no bus stop on that corner," the driver said.

"Well, the bus has *always*—"

"All them drivers breakin' the rules." The driver handed back a piece of paper to Dave. "You look under South Nyack on that list, you see Cedar Hill, Clinton, and Cornelison. Nothin' about no other stops."

"It seems to me—"

"Listen, man, give me a break. They call me up seven this mornin', tell me I has to work. You want to complain, talk to the boss."

"Maybe I'll do that," Dave said.

He walked back to where Anne was sitting, in the rear of the crowded bus. She had found the last vacant double seat. It was over the rear wheel, so that a large hump of black rubber, like a tumor in the floor, heaved up into the foot room of the seat near the window.

"Well, I guess I took care of that!" Dave said. He put the bags he was carrying up in the luggage rack and sat down next to Anne. "That son of a bitch will think twice before he passes somebody by again."

"Why don't you calm down a little bit?" Anne said. "Nothing terrible has happened, but you're getting into one of your states."

"Jesus, it's freezing in here," Dave said. "And somebody's smoking."

"Just relax and take a nap. We'll be home in no time." Anne squeezed against the window and rearranged the packages she was holding so that Dave would have more room. A large brown bag next to Dave swayed toward him, and a smaller brown bag at the top of the large one disgorged two green apples onto his lap.

"Jesus," he sighed. He leaned back and closed his eyes.

He was flying. He was skimming along south on Fifth Avenue, facedown, watching the cars and the lunchtime shoppers. He was completely naked. His altitude was about forty feet, and he was doing about fifteen miles an hour. People looked up and pointed. Traffic stopped. Dave decided to give his audience a treat; when he reached St. Patrick's Cathedral, he soared straight up at very high speed. He balanced himself on his right index finger atop one of the cathedral's spires, then feigned losing control and tumbled down like a movie mannequin. He stopped his fall about six inches above the sidewalk, rose once again to forty feet, and resumed his southward flight. Something pulled him to the left. He tried to compensate by flying to the right. He was pulled more sharply to the left, and he woke up. The bus had turned into a short side road, and was slowing down.

"Oh, no," Dave said. "Scouts."

"What?" Anne said.

"Look out the window. How many are there?"

"I can't see. What am I looking for?"

"Boy Scouts. There's a Scout camp at Alpine for city kids. They sometimes use this bus to get back and forth."

"Nothin' underneath?" someone outside the bus yelled.

"No, you got to bring your gear on up," the driver yelled back. "How many you got?"

"Twenty-five."

"Twenty-*five!*" Dave said.

"Well, come on," the driver shouted.

The boys started boarding the bus. Dave watched them as they made their way down the aisle. They were around eleven years old, and wore green shirts with red bandannas and red berets. Their enormous knapsacks were so wide that the boys had to take them off their backs and push or drag them along the floor. They were laughing and screaming at one another.

"Hurry up, José," one of them said to the first boy, a short, frail kid with the hugest knapsack Dave had ever seen. "I wanna get home so I can see you muhtuh on the Alpo ad tonight."

"Yeah, let's go, José," another boy yelled. "We got to get back in time for school tomorrow."

"Ease up!" José said. He got a death grip on his knapsack and wrestled it forward. He finally sat down in the aisle seat directly in front of Dave and with immense effort pulled the knapsack onto his lap.

The bus started to move, and the rest of the troop struggled to the rear, putting their equipment in the luggage rack if they could manage, and taking the few single seats that remained. More than fifteen had to stand, including what seemed to be the troop leader, a tall dark man with bad skin. There were red badges that said "Bronx 134" stitched on his sleeve.

All the boys had cascades of canteens, stopwatches, compasses, transistor radios, and brown-handled hunting knives almost the size of machetes—along with other gleaming metal items whose function Dave could not decipher— depending from various loops, strings, and belts on their uniforms.

"Which one is Hillary?" Dave said.

The presence of the Scouts in the aisle forced him to move farther into the seat, closer to Anne. He felt walled in by a forest of overdecorated Christmas trees. "In a Socialist system, Boy Scouts would have their own buses," he said.

"In a Socialist system, we'd all be Boy Scouts," Anne said.

"Hey, Tommy. Bet you can't wait to get to you house,"

yelled one of the boys who was standing. "You havin' roaches for dinnuh again?"

"Them roaches woulda been dead a long time if we could figure out which one was you muhtuh," someone replied from the row of seats that went the width of the bus at the very back.

"Doesn't anyone talk about lanyards anymore?" Dave said.

"They're having a good time," Anne said.

"First thing I'm a do is take my dog out for a walk," said a Scout standing near Dave.

"What's his name?" said another.

"Geraldo Rivera," said the first.

"My uncle's got a dog that's your big," said the other.

"Slick!" said the first.

As the bus drove through Englewood Cliffs, an instinctive musical urge seemed to sweep through the Scouts. Six or seven transistors were turned on at the same time. "WWRL," shouted one boy, and the rest tuned their radios to the same station.

> Come and get your love,
> Come and get your love,
> Come and get your love,
> Come and get your love,

The boys joined in singing, some doing the melody, some

doing their best with a bass part, and others high harmony.
The whole bus seemed to be swaying with the rhythm.

> Come-and-getcher-love, come-and
> getcher-love, come-and-getcher
> love now;
> Come-and-getcher-love, come-and
> getcher-love, come-and-getcher
> love now.

"Clever lyric," Dave said. He was fidgeting anxiously.
"Listen, I'm really getting claustrophobic."

"We'll be at the bridge any minute," Anne said.

"But the traffic will be awful; we'll never get there."

"I'm kind of enjoying it."

In Fort Lee, the bus slowed down. Dave looked across
Anne and out the window. The maze of arteries around the
George Washington Bridge was swollen with cars heading
home after the holiday. The bus inched along toward the
ramp it had to use to get on the bridge. The Scouts were still
singing, something about "let yourself go."

"It's going to be another half hour," Dave said. "We're
hardly moving."

Finally, the bus got down the ramp to the roadway that
led to the bridge. It crawled right, through three lanes of
nearly solid traffic, toward the bus stop just before the toll
booths.

"Is he going to put *more* people on this bus?" Dave said.

As the bus veered to take advantage of an opening, José leaned his head out over the aisle. His face wore a wan, apologetic look. He quietly vomited.

"Look out!" one of the standees said. "Hey, Mistuh Ramirez. José spit up."

"I tol' him not to eat all them Baby Ruths," said another one sagely.

"That's it! I'm getting off!" Dave said.

"What are you going to do—go across on the walkway?" Anne said.

"Exactly," Dave said. He pushed his way out onto the aisle. He leaned over and yanked the cord that ran along the sides of the bus and signaled to the driver that someone wanted to get off. "Are you coming with me, or are you just going to keep sitting there laughing?"

"You go on," Anne said. "Watch your step."

Dave snatched down from the luggage rack the bags that he had carried onto the bus. He shouldered past the Boy Scouts, toward the front of the bus, and reached the door just as it opened to let on a few people who were waiting at the stop. With a peremptory "Excuse me," he jostled them off the bus's two steps and finally reached the sidewalk.

Dave walked by hundreds of cars sitting virtually immobile on the broad plaza that lies on the other side of the toll barrier. Farther on, he saw that, after squeezing into the four or five eastbound lanes of the bridge proper, the traffic loosened up slightly and moved fitfully toward the Cross Bronx Expressway and the city itself. It was around six-thirty, he figured, and the homeward rush was beginning to peak. The cars seemed like an endless column of varicolored steel insects, shimmering in the heat, on their way to take over New York. Every now and then, they would scuttle forward a few feet, to fill in spaces created by their brothers in the vanguard, who half an hour earlier might have conquered a small new piece of territory at, say, Broadway and 113th Street.

Halfway across the bridge, hanging suspended between the states of New York and New Jersey, Dave felt the bottom of the bag holding the cut flowers give way. He looked down and saw that out of the corner that had soaked through and torn open was pouring a bunch of small seashells. These were followed by a dozen or so cherry tomatoes. Dave put all of his packages down. Then he got down on his hands and knees to pick up the shells and the tomatoes. He looked up for a moment at the traffic, which seemed suddenly to be moving quite fast. And as he looked up, he saw the No. 9-A Red & Tan bus go by, and he spotted Anne, still sitting in the same seat next to the window. He thought he saw, but could not be sure, that she had on her head a red beret.

Mole Hall

For a time I lived alone in one of the four first-floor apartments in the rear of a gigantic old building on Riverside Drive. It stood over the Drive on the crest of a hill just south of University Heights. Often when I went walking by the river, I looked up at the building where I lived and imagined it as a ship, especially in the wintertime. It was bravely fronting the wind that gathers force and consolidates over the Hudson and then hits the land in gusts like the shock waves of a bomb. In the summer, I imagined that with a word I could slice off the building's front wall, like the brown end of a roast, and that the tenants would have taken no notice. I could then have gone down to the park in the evening and watched a hundred compartmentalized, television-like dramas unfold simultaneously.

My apartment looked out on a dim, narrow courtyard bordered on three sides by other tall buildings and on one side, of course, by mine. It was a dignification to call that dismal rectangle of cement a courtyard. In the middle of it, two decrepit washing machines stood side by side—the kind with legs and casters on the bottom and crank wringers on the top. I thought of them as an old Jewish couple facing the final disaster together. Only a thin slice of sunlight reached down into the courtyard briefly each day, and even less found its way into my apartment.

Anyone who didn't know my place would probably have guessed from its location that it was a broom closet or a storage room. If the house was a ship, then I lived in aft steerage. My front doors (there were two—a regular heavy steel one, and one of what must have been the very few screen doors in Manhattan) were just to the right of my wing's freight elevator and at right angles to it. The passenger-elevator shaft stood beyond the one for the freight elevator. I could hear the machinery for the elevators working in the building's bowels, particularly at night, when daytime noises died down. The freight elevator's motor sounded like a muffled machine gun, and the one for the passenger elevator sounded like a faint, monotonous human whine. When the freight elevator's door and then gate opened on the first floor—which they often did during the day, to transport tenants down to or up from the laundry room in the basement —they made loud cracks, one hollow and distant, and the other sharp and metallic. Incoming and outgoing artillery. I could also hear the building's huge oil burners laboring below.

And, finally, the wind. There was a fifteen-foot gap between my building and the one south of it, and when a strong west wind forced its way through that gap at night, the noise was sometimes loud enough to keep me awake. It sounded the way I imagine a torrent of subatomic particles inside a cyclotron must sound. When the wind rushed across the courtyard this way, it created a partial vacuum along the back wall of the building, which seemed to suck the air out of my apartment. It took me a couple of weeks to figure out why I felt uncomfortable on windy evenings, and when I did figure it out, I immediately understood why my place had a screen door: to get any sort of ventilation, I had to open the metal door and, under these circumstances, the screen door although it had only a poorly seated hook-and-eye lock, provided at least a token barrier between my apartment and the stair landing at the rear of the lobby.

I slept very badly during the first week. But then, little by little, I adjusted. I grew accustomed to the noises, and I began to see coziness and privacy where I had originally seen only isolation. I noticed that the building's walls were thick and solid, though not completely soundproof. I saw that the paintings that hung in the lobby were surprisingly good, and that the floor there was marble. The management put down oriental rugs over the marble when cold weather came, and the brasswork on and around the entrance was kept gleaming.

Anne called my place Mole Hall. She hated it from the beginning and never changed her mind. Every time she walked in, she would look around like a movie prisoner of war who has just been pitched into his cell for the first time and is appraising his chances of escape. She would then often walk across the living room and look out the window, turning her face up to try to see the sky. "This place," she would murmur. I always asked her to spend the night, but she seldom did. She didn't like the idea of sleeping in a cave, she said. Her apartment had lots of sun in the morning, and waking up in the obscurity of my bedroom depressed her.

I think Anne was just generally angry with me in those days. She wanted to get married, or at least have me live with her, and I didn't want to—not right then. She had first brought the subject up when she was helping me move in to Mole Hall.

"You're too good for me," I told her as we were unpacking cartons in the living room. "I like professional wrestling on television, and I am overly concerned about occasional irregularity. If we got married, you would come to rue the day we met."

"I know all that," she said. "After two years, I know a lot. I don't happen to share your generally low opinion of yourself."

"I'm moody," I said. "I get angry. Even after only two or

three days together, you know how rotten I can get. You would hate me; I would be unbearable."

"Not if you made an effort—a commitment."

"I would feel trapped—"

"If you don't feel trapped in this place, you never will," she said.

"I would feel trapped and I would want to just get out," I said. "I mean, you give dinner parties. You have 'house guests.' You clip interesting items out of the newspaper and send them to friends who are living in Europe."

"We could compromise. We could learn to get along. It wouldn't kill you to try."

"I simply don't want to talk about it. I've just moved in here, and I'm going to stay here for a while."

"You know what I think?" she said. "I think you think you're too good for *me* and you won't admit it. You're afraid you would hate me."

"That, too," I said. "There are times when I can't stand anybody. Not anybody."

She dropped a small, squat ceramic troll that my mother had given me one Christmas. It shattered.

"Now look what you've done," I said. "You've broken my troll."

"I know," she said, "and he would have been so at home here."

From time to time after that, I would tease her by threat-

ening to paint my walls black and dwell in Mole Hall forever.

The building was big enough to require a staff of some
eleven or twelve full-time workmen. The three regular doormen were the ones I knew best, of course, though it was not
easy to carry on a conversation with any of them. John, a
tall black man, about sixty-five or seventy years old, who
worked in the morning and sorted the mail, was taciturn by
nature. Al, who manned the door in the afternoon and evening, seemed to be slightly retarded and repeated whatever
he said several times. A sad, drunken ex-cop named Fred
worked the midnight shift. He usually stopped mumbling to
himself only long enough to say good night when I came
home late. Eight or nine other men served variously as por-
ters, handymen, and so forth. My favorite among them was
Roland, a grotesquely fat porter. He wore a golden fez and
drove a Chevrolet convertible, and he fell asleep instantly
wherever and whenever he sat down. Over the three years I
lived there, Roland saw me leaving my place in the morning
in the company of girls other than Anne, and when he did
not call me "sir" he called me "you young rascal."

The man who presided over this crew was Mr. Herzig, the
superintendent. Presided under them, I should say, for he
and his family lived in the basement, directly below my
apartment. I thought of them as underground aborigines.

Mr. Herzig was squat and had long, apelike arms, and he
always wore pants and shirts of industrial green. This color

heightened the extreme floridness of his complexion. Almost every time I saw him he was angry. He yelled at his men—especially Roland—for being lazy, which made them try to get away with as much as they could. He greeted complaints by the tenants with truculence. And when he had to fill in for one of the doormen, who seemed to fall ill in a rotation nearly as regular as their work shifts, Mr. Herzig treated visitors the way a sentry might treat infiltrators.

One morning, not long after I moved in, I forgot to lock my door when I left for work. Mr. Herzig was waiting for me in the lobby when I got home that evening.

"You didn't lock your door this morning," he said, not looking at me.

"Jesus, what an idiot I am," I said.

"Anybody could have walked right in," he said.

"Well, I hope nobody did," I said.

"What are you trying to say?"

"Nothing," I said. "I didn't mean anything. I just hope nothing is missing."

"You have to be pretty stupid to forget something like that," he said.

"Jesus Christ, it's my door," I said. "Anyway, how did you know it wasn't locked?" I walked away before he could answer.

A couple of weeks later, I found him waiting for me in the lobby once again. He had discovered that I had given a set of keys for my apartment to Mrs. Dixon, who came in once a week to clean.

"I've worked with them all my life," he said. "You can't trust them."

"Listen," I said. "I have known Mrs. Dixon all *my* life. She was employed by my family before I was born, she took care of me when I was a child, and she has cleaned for me ever since I've had a place of my own. I trust her as much as I trust anyone in the world."

After several more genial conversations like these, I started to avoid Mr. Herzig whenever I could. If something needed fixing in my apartment, I either did it myself or, when I could, let it go.

I often wondered how Mr. Herzig had managed to find a wife. I imagined they had met in a dismal grotto somewhere, or at least in the subway. Mrs. Herzig was tall and wide, and gave the impression of being out of focus. She had, understandably, a look of almost total defeat. I say "almost" because she always wore daffy bright-red lipstick, which extended nearly out to her cheeks, up to her nose, and down to her chin. There were two sons. One was six or seven, pasty, and cunning. Mrs. Herzig often took him shopping with her on Saturdays, and whenever I saw the two of them emerging from the freight elevator, I always thought of a whale and her calf breaching for air. The older son was about sixteen. He seemed to have dropped out of school, and in the evenings I often saw him and a black kid with a huge Afro drinking beer on the corner of Broadway and glowering at passersby. At night, he often listened to a stereo set in what I guessed was his bedroom, right beneath the little room where I watched television and had my desk and books. He turned the volume up high enough for me to pick out some of the lyrics in the disco music he seemed to favor. He liked to play the same song over and over again— fifteen or twenty times in a row. The sound rose into my place like some muted, infernal mantra. The Herzigs had three German shepherds; I was told that they patrolled the basement corridors late at night. I sometimes saw the older son walking the dogs in Riverside Park. They would growl, bare their teeth, and pull against their leashes if anyone got too near. "Don't worry," the boy said to me once. "They just want to play."

At least once a month, usually on a Sunday night, the Herzigs would have a fight. It often started with Mr. Herzig bellowing abuse at the older son. His voice would rise above even the thundering from the stereo's speakers. Mrs. Herzig would scream at him to leave the boy alone. Then the door to the son's room would slam, and the shouting between Mr. and Mrs. Herzig would continue in what I assumed was their living room, right below mine. "Get out, you cocksucker, get out!" she would wail. Then would come a thump or a crash, followed by a moan from Mrs. Herzig or barking and howling from the dogs. Then more bumps and thuds and doors slamming, with contrapuntal shouts and curses. Finally, I would hear the staccato report of the freight elevator's motor. The gate and door would be thrown open with great violence, and Mr. Herzig would stalk out—whether in defeat or victory I never knew. When these fights took place I would turn my TV set off and follow the action from room to room, like Horatio trying to find the elusive ghost in the first scene of *Hamlet*.

One evening in the middle of June, Anne was visiting me when a battle broke out belowstairs. It startled us—me because it lacked the customary stereo overture. A door slammed, something that sounded as if it was made of glass shattered, and Mrs. Herzig began to shriek.

"What's going on?" Anne said.

"Listen to this," I said, getting down on the living room floor and putting my ear to it. "This is what I've been telling you about. It's incredible."

"I threw them away last night," I heard Mrs. Herzig yell. Mr. Herzig's voice was too low in pitch for me to catch his reply. Whatever it was, it caused Mrs. Herzig to resume shrieking. Then, suddenly, she stopped, and the fight seemed to be over.

"What do you suppose she threw away?" I said. "Do you suppose they were once desperately in love? Do you suppose she was smitten by his green uniform?"

"Do you suppose you could get up from the floor?" Anne said. "Honestly. If you're so interested in fights, we could always have one of our very own."

"That's what I'm afraid of," I said.

"I know," she said. She went over to the window.

"'This place,'" I said.

"This place, is right," she said.

"'You'd be a lot happier if—'" I said.

"Now, cut it out; you *would*. It's like you're hibernating."

"Aestivating," I said.

One evening at the end of July, I came home from work and found an unsealed envelope in front of the door to my apartment. A xeroxed note inside said:

> Our superintendant Mr. Herzig is in the hospital with abdominal surgery. The operation was a week ago. We of the tenents' association would like to help the Herzig family during this troubled time, and we have decided that a gift of money would be the most appropriate. If you desire, please put your contribution in an envelope along with your name and apartment No. and slip it under my door.
>
> Esther Gutmacher 16A
> Chair person
> Tenents' Association

I wasn't sure how much I really desired, but before I went to work the next morning I took the elevator up to 16 and pushed my contribution over the sill into 16A. I had to poke around among what I guessed must be other contributions before I found room for my own.

On my way out of the building, I asked John if he knew how Mr. Herzig was getting along.

"He got a catherter in his penis," John said, with Delphic solemnity.

"But he's getting better?" I said.

"All I know is he got a catherter in his penis."

On a sweltering Sunday afternoon two weeks later, Anne and I went to a movie at the Olympia Theater, on 107th Street and Broadway. It was only the second time we'd seen each other in six weeks. For a while, she had tried to get me to spend weekends with her in Quogue, on Long Island. She was friends with a married couple who owned what she called a "cute" house in Quogue, and they had told her to come out anytime.

"Quogue?" I had said when Anne first invited me. "Who would live in a place called Quogue? It sounds like a folk appellation for a serious stomach disorder. 'I'm sorry, Mrs. Mastodon, but I must inform you that little Jenny has a rather severe case of stychomythia.' 'But, Doctor, I never heard of that disease.' 'Yes you have, Mrs. Mastodon. You know it as—quogue!'" "What does Appalachia have to do with it?" Anne had said. "Appalachia?" I said. "You said 'Quogue' sounded like a folk Appalachian." "Yes, well," I said. "You see, the illness has been confined to Appalachia up until now. That's why I'm so surprised to hear about this outbreak on the Island, and that's why I don't want to go."

After a while, Anne stopped inviting me for these week-ends, and I pretty much stopped asking her to Mole Hall, because she simply wouldn't come any more.

"What now?" I said as we stood outside the theater.

"Why don't we go get something to eat?" Anne said. "We have to have a talk."

"We do?" I said.

"We have to settle things. This is getting ridiculous."

"It is?"

"Cut it out," she said. "You've got to make a decision about me."

"I don't got to do anything," I said. "Except my laundry. Come to my place and we'll talk over a hot cup of Clorox."

"I am not going to that crypt," she said. "I can't stand it. And I'm not going to see you again until you make up your mind." She turned and walked away.

"Irritability is the first symptom of quogue," I called after her, but she kept walking.

I stood there for a few minutes and then decided to go home. From the corner of 110th Street and Broadway, I saw Mrs. Herzig helping her husband out of a taxi in front of our building. Mr. Herzig was wearing his usual industrial green. When I reached the entrance, Al, the nearly retarded after-noon doorman, was standing on the steps. He jerked his thumb back toward the lobby and grinned.

"Yeah, I know," I said. "I saw him."

"Mr. Herzig just came back from the hospital," Al said.

"Yes, Al."

"He don't look too good," Al said, still grinning.

Indeed he didn't. He was sitting alone in the cool, dim lobby. He seemed dazed. He appeared at least thirty pounds lighter, and his face had lost much of its color. I didn't much want to talk to him, but I did anyway, to be polite.

"How are you feeling?" I said.

"Oh, I'm all right now, I guess," he said.

"It must be good to be out after a month," I said.

"I had two operations," he said.

"I didn't know that."

"The second one lasted six hours and I didn't come to for a whole day."

"Jesus, that sounds rough," I said.

"Two operations. You have to be pretty sick to get two operations in a month." He paused. "They tried to give me a nigger doctor," he said, more out of astonishment, it appeared, than outrage.

"Well, the important thing is that you're home now," I said, and turned to leave.

"Wait a minute," he said. I turned back to face him. "I wanted to say that we . . ." he said, not looking at me. "For the—well, for the—My wife and I appreciate it. That's all."

During the next month I found Mr. Herzig sitting alone in the lobby every morning when I left for work and every evening when I came home. He grew thinner and paler, as if he were in the process of fading out. His face became so white that I began to think of him as a marble gargoyle guarding the building's entrance. He nodded and smiled weakly as tenants went by. I heard no more fighting from the Herzig apartment, and the older son seemed to have stopped playing his stereo—which, I confess, was a relief.

Then one Saturday in the middle of September he was gone.

"They took him to the hospital early this morning," John told me. "I just started my shift," he said, "when here come Mrs. Herzig and her boys out of the subway. I saw them all the way down the block. She was crying. When she come up to me, she say, 'He's dead, John, he's gone.' Then she put her arms around me and just kept crying."

"Well," I said, "I might be wrong to say this, but I would have thought she'd be glad to be rid of him."

"You go on think what you want, boy," John said. "I got to look to the mail."

It was a beautiful, clear morning—a precursor of fall. A cold front had pushed through overnight, just as the weatherman on Channel 2 had said it would. I went to the park to try to get a pickup game of softball. Eventually, a game coalesced between two teams made up of random Columbia students, Puerto Ricans wearing baseball cleats, career girls in cutoff jeans, and shiftless bachelors like me.

Afterwards, as I walked up out of the park, I looked back down at the dirt-and-crabgrass field we had been playing on. A new game had started, between teams just as patched together as ours had been. Beyond and below the diamond ran the two cement stripes of the West Side Highway, beyond that lay the wide blue band of the Hudson, and beyond that loomed the long facade of the Jersey palisades, surmounted by high-rise apartment houses too big for their setting. They looked like monsters in silhouette, coming up from the flatlands and regrouping on high ground for a march on the city. In front of me was a narrow strip of park, beyond that Riverside Drive, then the Drive's narrow feeder road, and, finally, the wall of buildings on the hill. The brilliant air made everything look brittle and sharp, and the whole scene suddenly seemed to me permeated with surreal dread. I imagined that eons ago some giant had stood at the site of the George Washington Bridge with these various swaths of landscape rolled up in huge rolls and had unfurled them southward, as if he were installing carpets.

When I got back to my place, the stereo was on downstairs—louder than I had ever heard it before. I turned on my television; nothing was on but old movies and golf tournaments, and I could barely hear the sound above the roar from below. "Creepy kid," I said to myself. I turned the set off and tried to read, but the noise was too distracting. I looked for a movie in the paper, but I had seen everything that was playing in the neighborhood.

Finally, I picked up the phone and dialed Anne's number. I was surprised when she answered. "Is this you?" I said.

"Not if it's you," she said. "I'm not speaking to you."

"Then why did you call?" I said.

"Cut it out," she said. "Why did you call?"

"I want to move," I said. "Will you help me?"

There was a short silence.

Finally, she said, "Yes."

"And for God's sake don't break anything," I said.

Accommodations at Uncle Sol's

In a magnificent farmhouse just outside Great Barrington, Massachusetts, lives my father's elder brother, Uncle Sol. He is seventy-seven years old and a spry, gnomish bald man with big ears and a big nose. I don't know where he gets his money from, what there is of it. I do know that he is an old "progressive" from way back, that he subscribes to the *Daily World*, and that he speaks constantly of the "holocaust" or "catastrophe" that he sees lying in wait for us around the next turn in history. When he was younger, Uncle Sol worked as a labor organizer in New York City and earned a reputation among his friends and family for helping people —especially young people—when they lost their way or their job or the knack of just getting along. When I was a child, my parents sent me and our maid Wreatha to Uncle Sol's every summer, to get away from the city's polio epidemics and parochial-school children. I still love him and I still go to his place for one week every summer, by myself, during my vacation.

This summer, Uncle Sol said to me the night I arrived, "I just can't handle all the work around this place. I'm tired as a dog. Of course, I really don't care how the place looks anymore, but I think I'll go over to Pittsfield and see if I can't get this boy Larry to help me."

The next day, he drove away in the morning and returned at noon with Larry riding in the front seat. Larry is the son of Ethel, Uncle Sol's former cook and housekeeper. He is fourteen years old, a frail boy, very black. Uncle Sol put him right to work scraping the huge white double doors of the horse barn, which were badly in need of painting.

"I had to get that boy out of Pittsfield," Uncle Sol said to me as Larry went to work. "It's no good for him to be in the city with nothing to do. God knows I owe that much to his mother. She has helped me more than anyone." We stood in the driveway and watched Larry, who in two or three minutes reduced his attack upon the doors to bemused pickings interspersed with intricate and rather accomplished rhythms of the metal scraper against the aging wood.

I went and got another scraper from the shop and set to work helping Larry. The job was particularly hard, since there were three older layers of paint which adhered stubbornly to the wood even though they were cracked and blistered. Larry, whom I hadn't seen since my week at Uncle Sol's the summer before, started a conversation.

"You know them tractor-trailers, Davey," he said.

"Yeah."

"I *like* them tractor-trailers, man. The truckers over in Pittsfield, they let me go with them on some trips into New York State. You set real high off the road."

"Do you want to be a truck driver?" I asked.

"Yeah, man. You could make some money."

There was silence.

"Say, Davey, is that where you live, over in New York?"

"Yes. In the city."

"You mean where all them streets and lights is?"

"Yeah."

"You know, man, it's good to go and see different places," he said quite gravely. "It's good to get out of Pittsfield sometimes."

In the living room, later the same day, Uncle Sol was talking to Ella. She is my second cousin—technically in the same generation as me—but is over seventy. During the winter, Ella lives alone in the Bronx on her schoolteacher's pension. Her mother ran one of those green newsstands in Manhattan after her father abandoned the family. She put Ella through college, is the famous story. Every summer Ella comes to stay at Uncle Sol's. She tries to help him in the gardens and cleaning up the house, and she gets quite a bit done, considering that she is blind in one eye, partly sighted in the other, and almost deaf. In fact, she is very helpful and beats everyone at Scrabble.

"You know, he is very expensive to keep here," Uncle Sol was shouting at Ella. I had come in from the horse barn, Larry and I having finished all the scraping that was possible without splitting off wood underneath. I got some iced tea and sat down in the living room.

"And I just can't count on him to be around when I need him," Uncle Sol said. "I'd rather hire a reliable man and pay him." Ella, who pretends to hear more than she does, moved her head around in a strategic gesture that was neither yes nor no. Uncle Sol was speaking of Tom Guillermin, a young man from California who had somehow come to live at the farmhouse last winter as a kind of caretaker and stayed on in the summer in a corn crib that he had converted into sleeping quarters. "I think he has turned surly," Uncle Sol continued. "He has met so many girls and he goes off on dates and I never know when he'll be here." Ella bobbed. "You know, he broke the lawn mower a week ago. He cuts the grass like a wild man, he's in such a hurry to get through. He doesn't watch for rocks. He didn't tell me about breaking it; I had to find out for myself. Don't you think it's like a child, not telling me about something like that? When I gave it to Segalla, he told me that something had busted because the mower had been misused."

"When will it be ready?" I asked.

"It should be ready now," Uncle Sol said.

"Why don't I drive over to Canaan and get it?"

"Oh, Davey, you don't have to; you're supposed to be on vacation."

"I don't mind," I said. "I'll even put some blankets down in the back of your station wagon, so the mower won't scrape."

"You needn't bother with the blankets."

"In that case, I won't bother with the blankets."

"In that case, you'd better."

When I picked up the lawn mower at Segalla's, I asked the manager if the damage had come from mishandling. "Oh, no," he said. "This kind of breakdown just comes from heavy use. The summer has been wet, and the lawns grow like wildfire. We've had a lot of cases like this."

The next morning, Ella and I were in the kitchen having breakfast. Larry had already eaten and was outside knocking off blossoms with jets from the garden hose. As long as I can remember, Larry has loved playing with the hose, whipping its streams across the gardens and lawns as if he meant to punish them. Uncle Sol slept late; he often has great trouble getting to sleep, and reads into the early morning hours. Ella wandered around the kitchen picking abstractedly at some food in a bowl. Some cottage cheese had gotten stuck on her nose. I was trying to make some waffles on an old iron. The batter kept sticking to the iron. Finally, a fuse blew.

"God damn it," I said.

"What?"

"I said this God-damned waffle iron thinks it's a Stradivarius."

Ella bobbed. "Are you going to cook some waffles?"

"I blew a fuse," I yelled.

Suddenly, Tom appeared in the doorway. "Where have *you* been, Mister?" Ella asked as she walked out of the kitchen.

"Hi, Tom," I said. "Uncle Sol is mad at you. I heard him telling Ella yesterday that you're never around when he needs you and that you're very expensive to keep."

"Expensive! What does he mean? He doesn't pay me anything, and all I do is have two or three meals a day when I'm here, and he can ask me to do anything he wants."

"Well, I don't know," I said. "I guess he doesn't have very much money and he really wants somebody to be at his elbow. You can't blame him. I just thought I'd tell you. Where were you—on a date?"

"Yeah. I went down to New York. I met this girl who runs the men's boutique at Bloomingdale's. She's a cousin of some friend of Sol's who has a place on Lake Buel Road, and they came over here for a visit a couple of weeks ago. Are you on vacation?"

"Yeah. What's this girl's name from Bloomingdale's?"

"Diane."

"So did you get anything?"

Tom laughed.

"Are you going to cook waffles?" he asked, looking at the gluey iron.

"I was going to, but the iron kept sticking and now I've blown a fuse."

"I'll fix it and show you how to work the iron. Your batter looks too thin, anyway."

Tom changed the fuse and came downstairs again to thicken the batter, which was in a cup. When he finished adding stuff to it, I poured it into a blender, but the white-yellow batter was so thick now that some of it stuck to the cup. I knocked the cup against the blender's glass container. It still stuck. I knocked the cup a little harder and cracked the container.

"Uh-oh," I said. "Don't tell Uncle Sol. I'll drive into Great Barrington this afternoon and try to replace it," I said to Tom. I buried the broken glass under some other trash in the garbage can and hid the base of the blender in a cranny.

Since I didn't know whether Uncle Sol wanted the barn doors painted right away, I went to work with Tom after breakfast, scraping the north side of the house itself. Tom's main work for the summer was painting the house, and he had it three-quarters finished. I had suggested the project to him during the winter, when I had come up to go skiing and met Tom for the first time. I had noticed that the house was peeling badly, and when Tom wondered out loud what he could do to earn his keep if he decided to stay for the summer, I assured him that once Uncle Sol got back from Mexico, where he was performing some mysterious "progressive" errands and taking care of his sinuses, he would find plenty that needed to be done. I suggested that painting the house would be a good place to start in the spring.

We stripped down for the job, since it was an oppressively hot day, with thunderclouds marching up from the south. I had never seen Tom without a shirt before. He had been a world-class pole-vaulter a few years back, and his athlete's body was nothing but knots of muscles. Soon Larry came to join us and started drumming on the house.

After an hour or so, I took a break and walked around to the front of the house. I found Uncle Sol regarding the barn doors like a general reviewing ragged troops.

"Good morning, Uncle Sol," I said. "Do you want the barn doors painted now? What kind of paint should we use, and where is it?"

"More paint needs to come off," he said.

"But if you take any more of the old paint off, rotten wood comes off with it. I think we should just go ahead and finish it. It'll look O.K."

"Listen, Davey, it's not that I don't appreciate what you do for me when you come up, but you just don't know about these things."

"All right," I said. "I'll try to get some more off." I got out the stepladder and set about hunting for overlooked scrapable sections. Uncle Sol went back into the house and lay down.

We all took another break at about three o'clock, and I snuck off into town with the blender base. "Why, that's a Sun Monarch," the man at the hardware store told me. "That's a real old blender and a good one. We don't have any replacements for that. You'll have to send to St. Louis— if they're still in business. Come on, Herb, look at this old Sun Monarch," he called to his helper. "I haven't seen one of these in fifteen years. It's a pity they're not around anymore."

"I'll say," I said. I decided not to mention the blender to Uncle Sol until I left, in a few days.

On the way back to the farmhouse, I stopped at a roadside stand and ordered a steak hero (they call them "subs" in Massachusetts), with the works, for lunch. It was delicious, but I could only eat half of it.

By the time I got back, the clouds had banded together into a sky of sullen lead. Uncle Sol was standing in the driveway. "What's that you got in your hand, boy?" he said as I walked toward him.

"Oh, half a steak sub," I said. "I was hungry."

"That's crazy. We would have fed you here; you know that. Why spend your money?"

"I'm on vacation, and I like to spend money on vacation," I said.

Uncle Sol smote his forehead with the heel of his hand.

Tom was wheeling the lawn mower out from the toolshed. "Better get the lawns before it rains," he said. "They're already like jungles." He had put the scrapers and ladders away. I went into the house and put the wrapped-up half hero in the refrigerator.

I've never seen anyone mow a lawn as Tom did that afternoon. He approached the nearly three acres of lawn that lie around the farmhouse as if they were foreign, hostile territories that had to be conquered and ruled with an iron hand. He laid out the various sections into subsections by cutting boundaries into them with the mower. He mowed so that all the grass was thrown toward the middle of a subsection, making Larry's and my raking and wheelbarrow loading quite easy. He had three caches of gasoline in three different outbuildings, each of them near a place where he knew he would run out. He mowed very quickly, taking the biggest possible swaths of lawn but never leaving any "holidays," as Uncle Sol called them—the narrow ridges of grass that result from too much ambition. He knew where every rock was and avoided each of them gracefully, leaving only a few tufts behind.

He had nearly finished the last section, in back of the house, when dusk finally started to fall. Ella rang the cowbell for supper, but Tom wanted to finish. Uncle Sol came out and told us to stop—that everything would get cold if we didn't. "I don't know why he won't let me take five more minutes," Tom said to me as we walked into the house. "He never lets me complete anything."

"You know, I don't know why nobody ever finishes anything around here," Uncle Sol shouted to Ella later that evening. Larry and Tom and I had gone to bed at about eleven, with the rain falling and the thunder making artillery rumbles in the distance. But I could hear Uncle Sol through the grate in my room, upstairs above the living room. "They got that door scraped and then put that aside and did the lawn. And he must have hit twenty rocks." I could almost hear Ella bobbing.

A little later on, I went downstairs for some aspirin. I found Uncle Sol in the kitchen, eating the rest of my steak hero.

A couple of days later, when I was leaving Uncle Sol's, he said to me in the driveway, "You know, you should have told me about that blender. I wanted to puree some tomatoes this morning for your momma down in Nyack. I couldn't find the container, and then Tom told me you'd broken it. Now, that was like a child, not telling me about it."

"Well, I was trying to replace it in town," I said. "I was

just about to tell you. I didn't see any point in upsetting you about it if there was no need."

"I'm not upset; you didn't need to worry about that," Uncle Sol said. "I don't mind when these things happen; I just want to know, that's all. Are you afraid of me, boy?"

"Yes."

"That's the craziest thing I've ever heard. You and I have never had any trouble."

On Monday, back in New York, before I went to my office, I stopped at Korvettes on Fifth Avenue. I bought an exquisite Osterizer blender, with so many buttons and dials on its front that it looked like the console of a jet fighter. I asked the salesman, Mr. Dubowsky, to have it sent to Uncle Sol's. Mr. Dubowsky had a bad cold and shreds of white Kleenex clung to his suit. "It's for his birthday," I explained to Mr. Dubowsky, who hadn't asked. "His birthday is in a few weeks, and I just thought he might be able to use a good blender. I heard Osterizer was the best."

"The best blender ever made," said Mr. Dubowsky, with a scholar's certainty, "was the Sun Monarch. They stopped making them about ten years ago, and nothing since then has come close."

The Three-Mile Hill
Is Five Miles Long

On Saturday at around noon, Dave and Anne left the ski slopes at Butternut Basin and drove back to Uncle Sol's farmhouse, where they were staying, for lunch. Dave said he didn't want to pay seventy-five cents at the ski lodge for a hamburger that looked to him as thin as a buzz-saw blade. Anne said that she had known that Dave would say that; he had said it the first time he had brought her to Uncle Sol's, a month ago. So she had made a lunch to take with them before they left the city Friday evening for the Berkshires. She had packed it in with the rest of the groceries for the weekend, and it was now sitting in Uncle Sol's refrigerator.

"What's in it?" Dave said.

"All your favorites," Anne said.

"What are my favorites?" Dave said.

"Peanut butter and jelly on Wonder Bread, Canada Dry ginger ale, Pepperidge Farm Milanos, and Cracker Barrel cheese—sharp," Anne said.

With his ski gear on, Dave could barely squeeze in and out of the driver's seat of his car. At the top of the driveway at Uncle Sol's, he heaved his legs out of the car and then popped the rest of his body out from under the steering wheel, feeling like a cartoon character. The rigid plastic ski boots he was wearing made his footing uncertain on the icy driveway, and as he tried to stand, he slipped and fell. He wasn't hurt, but he lay there anyway, staring at the cold, bright-blue February sky and at the black tree branches stacked with snow. When he and Anne were driving up the Taconic, the night before, the stars were out. The snow must have started after they went to sleep. When they woke up, a bright sun was shining and the Berkshires were dazzling with three or four inches of new snow. Dave found it disturbing that so great a change—the transformation of an entire countryside—had taken place while he was asleep.

Dave still did not get up. He lay there watching his breath form frost clouds, and he listened to the pulse pumping in his ears, steady and strong, as if it would go on forever. He heard the door to the farmhouse close. She'll go into the kitchen and take off her parka, he thought. She'll wash her hands, and as she washes her hands, she'll look out at the driveway to see what has happened to me. She won't be able to see me lying here, so she'll come out to look for me. She'll be slightly worried, but she'll also suspect that I'm just playing another trick on her. She'll find me here, ask if I'm O.K., and when she knows that I am, she'll wait for me to get up. "Come on," she'll say, "it's freezing out here."

He heard the door to the farmhouse close again. After a few seconds, Anne appeared around the front of the car. Dave smiled up at her.

"Did you hurt yourself?" she said.

"No," Dave said. "I'm just lyin' here, groovin' on the ice vibrations and the basic basicness of the cosmos. Can you dig it?"

"Come on, get up," Anne said.

"Aren't you going to say it's freezing out here?"

"It's not bad in the sun. But I'm starving. Come on."

The door to Uncle Sol's house opened directly into the dining room, which had large windows at the far end and cherry-wood paneling and a long mahogany table in the center. To the left was the kitchen, and to the right the living room, and, beyond that, Uncle Sol's bedroom. Five more bedrooms were upstairs. The original building had been erected in the seventeen-nineties, and as it and the land changed hands over the years, it grew, as if, Dave thought, it were alive. Like many other New England farmhouses, it now resembled a telescope set down horizontally on the ground, with the smallest section in the rear and the largest fronting the road.

Dave sat on one of the dining room chairs struggling to get his boots off. He stopped for a moment and looked around. The house was quiet. Uncle Sol had left for Mexico to nurse his sinuses a few days before, so Dave and Anne had the place to themselves. Dave looked at the floor and noticed for the first time that its boards were not of uniform width. Centuries, he thought; you could almost say that this house had existed for centuries.

"Somebody stole our lunch," Anne shouted from the kitchen.

"Who?" Dave said.

"'Who?'" Anne said. "What do you mean 'Who?'"

"Well, where is it?" Dave said.

"I'm telling you it's gone. Somebody must have taken it. I put it in a separate bag in the refrigerator, and the bag is gone."

"You shouldn't put peanut butter stuff in the refrigerator," Dave said. "It gets rigid." He had finally gotten his boots off, and he went into the kitchen.

"It was right there," Anne said. She was standing next to the open refrigerator, gesturing toward it like Betty Furness.

"Hello," said a reedy and tremulous voice behind them.

They both jumped a little and turned around. Standing in the doorway between the kitchen and the dining room was a short, stocky man wearing brown corduroy pants, a soiled plaid shirt, an ancient pea jacket, and a blue baseball cap with the New York Mets' insignia on it. In his hand was an empty ginger ale bottle. He had blue eyes, a prominent hook nose, and large ears. He looked like Dave transformed from thirty-three to eighty-three.

"Uncle Nick!" Dave said. "I thought you were in New York. You startled us."

"Hello, Robert," the old man said, smiling pleasantly. "I was upstairs taking a nap."

"I'm Dave—your nephew," Dave said.

"Why are you shouting?" Anne said.

"He's almost deaf," Dave said softly. "I'm Dave," he shouted again. "Bob is your brother—my father."

"Oh, yes," the old man said. "David." He looked at Anne. "You are the young woman from the South."

Anne smiles. "What is he talking about?" she whispered to Dave.

"No, Nick," Dave yelled. "That was someone else. This is Anne Springer."

"Pleased to meet you, Anne," said Uncle Nick.

"Uncle Nick, did you eat our lunch that was in the bag in the refrigerator?" Dave boomed.

The old man said, "I have sold a book for seventy-two million dollars. I am already working on a second one. They say they will give me more for the second one. The one they have already bought is about my son's psychoanalysis. I paid fifty thousand dollars for my son's psychoanalysis." He came into the kitchen a few steps and put the ginger ale bottle in the kitchen sink.

"Uncle Nick," Dave said, "are you staying at the Chicken House?"

The old man went back and stood in the doorway. "Yes," he said.

"But you have no heat, I thought."

"Heat, but no hot water. I've been walking up here to use the water."

"Where's your car?"

"They took my license away."

"How did you get up here?"

"I came up from the city last week. I took a bus and then a taxi out from town."

Dave closed the refrigerator and walked over to where Uncle Nick stood. "Let me drive you back to the Chicken House," he said, putting his hand on the old man's shoulder.

"I have to get the camp ready," Uncle Nick said. "A lot of work needs to be done. I've got all the counselors lined up, and my wife, Ruth, is recruiting boys in New York."

"I thought you told me that your Aunt Ruth was dead," Anne said to Dave when he got back from the Chicken House.

"She is," Dave said. "She died ten years ago. The Boys Camp has been closed ever since." He paused. "Listen, let's drive into Great Barrington and go to MacDonald's."

"O.K.," Anne said. "If you really prefer shredded compressed something to buzz-saw blades."

They put on their coats and went outside.

Dave backed the car out of the driveway. They drove for a mile or so in silence, and then Anne said, "Why does he live in a chicken house?"

"*The* Chicken House," Dave said. "After Aunt Ruth died, Nick couldn't handle the camp by himself. He sold their house but kept the land and the camp. He renovated part of an old chicken house and moved in there. He also has an apartment in New York. I thought he was there." He paused. "Don't ask me," he said. "I don't know."

Dave slowed the car to make a left turn on to Route 23. They started down the long hill that leads into Great Barrington.

"The Three-Mile Hill is five miles long, doo-dah, doo-dah," Dave sang, to the tune of "Camptown Races."

"What is that," Anne said.

"A family ditty about this hill," Dave said. "When Uncle Sol sings it, he always says, 'Doo-dah, singee doo-dah.'"

"I don't understand your family," Anne said.

"Neither do I."

"Tell me what you know," Anne said.

"Someday," Dave said.

They drove past Butternut Basin.

"The slopes," Dave said. "Did you see how beautiful it was at the top today?"

"But who takes care of him?" Anne said.

"He had an operation last summer, for varicose veins. His mind hasn't been right since then, Uncle Sol told me. Nobody takes care of him, I guess. Who knows? Perhaps he is fiercely independent. With seventy-two million dollars, he can certainly afford to be."

"Don't make fun of him," Anne said.

"Listen," Dave said, "when I drove him to the Chicken House, he made me guess how much his shoes cost. It turned out he bought them at a thrift shop and they cost a quarter. In the very next breath, as they say, he told me he had made them himself—out of doeskin."

"Why do you try to make all this into a joke?" Anne said.

"Who's laughing?" Dave said.

Dave turned into the MacDonald's parking lot. "The golden arches," he said. "An oasis of sanity." He parked and turned off the motor. "Don't get out yet," he said. "Listen, it's just that the whole thing makes me feel a little on the precarious side."

"I could tell that," Anne said. She put her hand on his shoulder and leaned over and kissed his cheek.

They skied again in the afternoon until the lifts shut down, at five. At the end, Dave took one of his gloves off and put it in the inside pocket of his parka. He and Anne skied over to the main chair lift, where the operator had just started turning people away. The lift was still running, however, so that the last people aboard could get to the top. Dave told the operator that he had lost one of his gloves, and couldn't he please go up to look for it. The operator said O.K. Anne decided she was too tired for another run, and said that she would wait for Dave in the car.

After Dave got off the lift, he put on his other glove. Then he turned left and skied slowly down a gentle, narrow trail that went across the top of a ridge and fed into the slope he wanted. He was alone, and everything was still. Below and in the distance, he could see small towns and clusters of houses, and tiny, bright-colored automobiles that scooted like bugs along roads that looked like thin, gray scars. The hills were white, and the pines stood up from them like green armies. Closer by, he heard a mountain stream rushing. An owl hooted. Crepuscular, Dave thought.

He started down the slope. He pretended that he was a soldier in the Finnish ski troops during the Second World War. He was on his way to rescue a wounded comrade lying at the foot of the mountain. If he didn't get there fast, the Russians would cut him off, which would spell certain death for both of them. He skied much faster than he did ordinarily, and took some dangerous risks. When he reached a large mogul that he usually avoided, he went directly over it and flew for a few yards in the air. He slapped his skis down on the snow harder and louder than he needed to when he landed, and he bent his knees more than was necessary to cushion the impact.

Then the trail bent and the parking lot appeared below. Dave came to a stop. It was unlikely, he reflected, that the Russians would have arrived in a fleet of Volvos.

When Dave and Anne got back to Uncle Sol's, Dave searched the house. "He's not here," he reported to Anne, who was lighting the fire in the living room fireplace. "But what if he comes back?"

"What if he does?"

"To use the water," Dave said.

"Just forget about him," Anne said. "Listen, will you cook? I want to take a shower."

"I would be glad to," Dave said. "Provided my grandfather hasn't come back from the grave and stolen our supper."

They ate in front of the fire while watching what Anne called "the programs"—Mary Tyler Moore and Bob Newhart—on the TV set that Dave had taken out of Uncle Sol's bedroom. Dave rated all the jokes. "*That's* funny," he would say, or "Average," or "Fair," or "Weak, very weak." Anne kept telling him, "Hush. Keep still."

"'Hush. Keep still,'" Dave said. "Nobody says that anymore."

As it got later, Dave felt more and more relaxed. He and Anne had nearly finished a bottle of wine that Dave had found in Uncle Sol's room behind the TV. He cleared away the dishes. He came back to the living room, put a log on the fire, and sat down next to Anne on the couch. Bob Newhart was trying to convince his wife that flying was nothing to be afraid of.

"Let's do something," Dave said.

"I don't know if I can resist you when you are so romantic," Anne said.

"Come on," Dave said.

"I want to watch the programs," Anne said.

"Why doesn't Suzanne Pleshette do something about her hair?" Dave said. "It's a question that is now on the lips of many Americans."

Anne laughed and put her head on his shoulder.

Dave heard the front door open.

"Oh, dear," Anne said. "Listen, just try to ignore him."

Uncle Nick appeared in the doorway between the dining room and the living room. His baseball cap was on backward. "Hello," he said. "I need to take a bath."

"Go ahead," Dave shouted.

The old man stood in the doorway for a minute or so, looking at the fire and the television and Dave and Anne as if, Dave thought, he were a tourist. Then he crossed in front of them and went into the small bathroom between the living room and Uncle Sol's bedroom. They heard the water start to run in the bathtub.

"Why couldn't he have gone upstairs?" Dave said.

"It won't take long," Anne said. "Finish the wine."

After a few minutes, the water stopped running. A few

minutes later, mumbling sounds started coming out of the bathroom. Then the old man started shouting. "Give me back that money!" he yelled. "I did not give you ten dollars, I lent it to you. You won't get away with this! You owe me ten dollars."

"Jesus," Dave said.

"Robert," the old man yelled. "Come in here and help me. This man is trying to steal my ten dollars."

Dave got up and went into the bathroom. The old man sat in the bathtub gripping the wooden rim that went around the top.

"Nick, you must have gone to sleep and had a dream," Dave said.

"What?" the old man said.

"I'm Dave—your nephew. Everything is O.K. You must have dozed off in the water. Nobody took any money."

"David," the old man said. "I thought he stole ten dollars from me." He pointed toward his pea jacket, which was hanging on top of the rest of his clothes on a towel rack.

"Nobody's in here but you and me," Dave said. "Why don't you dry off and get dressed." He looked at his uncle, who had now calmed down. His body was very white in the tub, but he seemed in remarkably good shape. Only his face looked old. Tears came to Dave's eyes. "You get dressed," Dave said. "I'll be right outside." He went back out into the living room.

"Jesus," he said to Anne. "He thought his coat was a person."

"He'll be gone soon," Anne said, "and he won't be back tonight." She took Dave's arm. "Sit down," she said.

After a short time, the bathroom door opened. Uncle Nick stood in the doorway, fully dressed except for his cap, which he held in his hands.

"I'm very sorry," he said. "I can't imagine what came over me."

Dave felt a great sense of relief. "Don't worry about it, Uncle Nick," he said. "I told you: You were just dreaming."

"I simply didn't realize that he was colored," the old man said. "If I had seen that he was colored, I would have let him keep the ten dollars. I don't care about money."

It started to snow that night when they were halfway down the Taconic. The flakes were big and ragged, and looked to Dave like flakes of paint scraped from an immense ceiling. The snow reduced his visibility, so he had to slow the car down.

"I told you we should have waited till tomorrow to drive home," Anne said. "The skiing would have been fantastic tomorrow, and the driving is dangerous tonight."

"If he had gone back to the Chicken House, if he hadn't fallen asleep in that chair, I would have stayed."

"Why couldn't we just go to bed and pay him no attention?"

"You know, he always claimed to be a Marxist. He was embarrassed about how successful the camp was. At the end, he had a hundred and fifty rich Jewish boys from New York at about fifteen hundred dollars a throw. Along with a few token blacks. When I was a kid, I used to hear him say things like 'Every cent goes back into the land,' and 'Ruth and I live on thirty-three hundred dollars a year.'"

"He would have just slept there," Anne said.

"Listen," Dave said, "if we had gone to sleep, what if he started shouting again downstairs? What if he went chasing thieves through our bedroom? No thanks."

"I think he liked our company."

"Oh, I'm sure plenty of people will be dropping in on him."

"There you go again," Anne said.

"Listen," Dave said, "I don't like things creeping up on me when I'm not looking."

The Champion

My brother, his two trainers, and my wife, Elizabeth, and I live together in a huge loft in an old part of this city. The loft, which takes up the entire floor of a time-blackened industrial building, must once have housed a business of some sort, because the upper half of the wooden door that opens into it consists largely of a panel of frosted, nearly opaque glass—the kind of panel that often bears the name of a company. Our accommodations here are crude. We sleep on mattresses on the floor. There are no rooms, or even partitions—just a vast, L-shaped open space. The kitchen and bathroom, such as they are, are located in the short leg of the L. The long leg has eight windows that look out on a narrow street, nearly always deserted. Every now and then, a single car or truck passes by; there are virtually no pedestrians. We live this way because my brother chooses to, and he is our life. He is the heavyweight champion of the world.

My brother once explained to me that he must remain a man of the people. Elizabeth frequently asks if she can't make the place a little nicer—touch up the paint or hang some curtains or buy some rugs—but my brother will not allow it. Obviously, he could have a mansion if he wanted one. He could have a plane, a yacht, dozens of cars, if he wanted them. But he does not want them, and how he uses the great sums of money he makes for defending his championship I do not know.

Recently, however, he has permitted himself one extravagance. After he signed for the bout with Griffin a while ago, I told him I could no longer bear to see him fight in person. So he had a thirty-foot-by-thirty-foot closed-circuit color television screen built into one of the loft's blank walls—the one at the blind end of the L's longer leg. He said that knowing I was watching him fight always gave him strength. Even if I watched him from the loft, it would do, he said. But I had to promise him that I would watch.

This morning, some technicians came in to run a final test on the television equipment, since the fight takes place tonight. It is being held in an outdoor stadium in New Delhi and will be telecast to theaters around the world. The only private showing will be the one in our loft.

All we could see on the screen at first were vertical pastel bands, and all we could hear was static. Then a crisp image of an empty boxing ring surrounded by empty seats snapped on, and a man's voice, heightened to nearly deafening volume said "Beautiful, oh, beautiful" over the speakers on either side of the screen. The technicians turned the speakers off and showed us how to turn them on again for when the fight started. The pictures, first from one camera position and then from another, panning here and zooming in there, have been flickering silently on the wall all day.

Many reporters have asked if they could cover the story of the fight from the loft, for a "human interest" angle. But I told my brother I did not want them here, so he would not allow it. This means that besides Elizabeth and me, only Vinnie, one of my brother's two trainers, will be here to see the bout. Vinnie has never gone to any of my brother's fights. He only trains him beforehand and takes care of his injuries afterwards. Luis, the other trainer, works during the fights. I do not know why my brother has arranged things this way, and I do not know why he has only the one man, Luis, in his corner between rounds. All the other boxers have three.

The telecast will start at nine o'clock. It is now eight, and Elizabeth has cooked supper for us, but I can eat nothing. This Griffin is a dangerous man—a squat, knot-muscled brawler, much younger than my brother. There was a time when none of us would have worried about Griffin. My brother assumed the championship when he was twenty-one, and for years he seemed invincible. His size, speed, and self-discipline set him apart from any heavyweight before him. There were many fights in which his only contest was against perfection. In those days, my brother and I would walk the streets of this city, and the boulevards and broad avenues of foreign cities, and people would crowd about him, clapping and cheering. Children ran after him and hung from his arms as if they were swinging from the limbs of a tree. Sometimes he would try to cast off his serious manner by feinting punches at the children. The intensity of their glee over this game always seemed to surprise him.

Now all that has changed. People make way for my brother, greeting him quietly as he goes by. They feel, as I do, that it cannot be much longer until he loses his title, and their love for him appears mixed with great foreboding, as is mine. Although he hits with as much power as he ever did—perhaps even more—he has slowed down, and his stamina is not what it was. He has become a precarious hero. The people cherish him more than ever, but they now also fear for him. He embodies the tragedy of time, and the people do not clamber to get near him, to touch him, as they once did.

The stadium is filled. The cameras scan the crowd, first with long shots, then with tighter ones. Almost all the spectators have straight black hair and dark eyes, and their faces are brown or mahogany or copper-colored. The few white men among them sit near ringside. The screen is like a window on the stadium, so perfect are the images. When I turn the sound on, the noise of the crowd fills the loft. An empty ramp appears on the screen. Five or six men enter the ramp at the far end and walk toward the camera. It is Griffin and his entourage. Now a different camera is cued in, showing a wide shot of Griffin walking down a long aisle and then climbing through the ropes. The crowd stirs only slightly. Another empty ramp appears. My brother, accompanied only by Luis, comes through it and into the stadium proper. Applause cascades down upon him and grows to a kind of white torrent. I fear for a moment that the noise will crush him. I notice that I am trembling. I am certain that he will lose.

The fight begins. At first, my brother manages to keep the stubby, clumsy Griffin at a distance, controlling the ring and waiting for his opponent's strength to flag, as a fisherman rides out the struggles of his catch until it weakens and can be landed. But Griffin does not weaken. In the middle rounds, he begins to break through my brother's defenses. When he gets inside, he hits my brother with repeated club-like blows to the body. My brother, usually expressionless when he fights, wears a look of faint puzzlement.

Griffin's confidence grows as the bout wears on. The crowd's roar subsides to a murmur, as if they were witnessing an agonizingly slow accident, and the directional microphones at ringside pick up clearly the thud of Griffin's blows. My brother remains proud and graceful even as he is being beaten. At the heart of the terror in the ring there lies a strange sort of beauty.

In the fourteenth round, Griffin's assurance decays into negligence. With less than a minute to go, he drops his gloves and straightens up, as if contemplating a nearly finished piece of work. My brother steps forward and lands a sharp left hook. As Griffin's head snaps to the side, my brother meets it with a straight right thrown from short range, like the stroke of a piston. The crowd cries out with one voice a fraction of a second after the blow's impact, and then falls silent, as if they too had been struck, while Griffin is counted out. The tension breaks, and the crowd roars in a tumultuous panic. The sound is unbearable. I ask Vinnie to turn the speakers off.

A camera catches a monumental close-up of my brother. His chest heaves and his face glistens with beads and streams of sweat. I am sobbing. Elizabeth holds me and tells me that it is all over. The camera pans back and shows the ring swarming silently with people, my brother standing in their midst.

It comes to me that I was hoping he would lose. Just to have it done with, to discover what will happen to us once the burden of his greatness is lifted away. I dread that he may never lose, that he will continue as champion forever, but at greater and greater cost, with more and more suffering.

People are clamoring at the door to the loft. It will be the press, wanting interviews and pictures. Vinnie goes to the door and opens it, and tells the reporters and photographers that he is sorry but he cannot let them in. He closes the door again, with some difficulty. Just before it is completely shut, I see that one photographer is pressing his camera against the thick glass panel, hoping, perhaps, to catch some shadow of an image from within. It occurs to me that getting close to a barrier as opaque as that pane will not clarify what lies beyond it at all.